ERIK

Guards of Clan Ross

USA TODAY BESTSELLING AUTHOR

ALSO BY HILDIE MCQUEEN

ERIK: GUARDS OF CLAN ROSS

This fictional story takes place at the beginning of the 17th century on South Uist—an isle of the Outer Hebrides, off Scotland's west coast.

Guards of Clan Ross is a spin-off series from Clan Ross of the Hebrides, which begins with *The Lion*. Enjoy!

If you would like to read *The Lion* first, here is the link: https://amzn.to/3vVqBUA

CHAPTER ONE

R IDING TO WHERE one could face death was not exactly
Erik Larsen's idea of a good day.

Two by two, the contingent of Ross warriors, archers and
helpers rode southwest to an area that up until recently had
remained unfamiliar to them. Since taking over lairdship,
Laird Darach Ross had only visited once, briefly, the tiny
villages and farms that dotted the hilly landscape.

Newly charged with leadership, Erik Larsen scanned the
surroundings, assessing the possibilities of any danger. The
people of the area had brought a grave situation to Laird Ross'
attention and were anxious for help.

Just past the villages of Asbury and Welland—which belonged to Clan Ross, was a remote and isolated large village
called Creag. There was a lush forest with a creek that ran
through it that formed a natural boundary between the two
borders. This creek had always been peaceably shared by both
the Ross people and the inhabitants of Creag.

Then people—Ross people—began disappearing, others
were injured, and several had been killed. Those that survived
told of archers shooting down from trees, of men with thick
wooden rods and swords attacking and robbing them.

Erik turned to his second. "The land is plentiful. I do not
understand the need to hurt people for a meager reward of a

deer, or a rabbit."

"One young man was purposefully released without injury and told to return to his village and inform the people that the forest is forbidden territory," Torac replied.

"Then it is about the land than what they can possibly acquire," Erik added with a grunt. "The idiots must be aware of the Clan Ross' power. They stand no chance against us."

Torac nodded. "And yet our laird only sends a small contingent. He is honoring a decades old treaty. An agreement between us and them to not battle."

Obviously, the inhabitants of the village were not adhering to the treaty. Erik had been about to ask the laird why Clan Ross why they were keeping the treaty when it wasn't being honored by the others, but he had been interrupted by abrupt orders to mount and prepare to take their leave.

The light rain, continued steadily, pelting down on him and his men. Along with the rain came a chilled salty wind as they were near the western shore. Erik pulled his fur cape tighter around his shoulders and set his jaw.

He guessed their destination was another day's ride and did not look forward to continuing to ride in the rain. As if in revolt, dark clouds gathered, and the rain became heavier.

"God's foot," Erik muttered, shaking the rain from his long blond hair. "We need to find a dry place to camp for the night."

A scout rode toward him, the young man looking as miserable as Erik felt. "There is a cave like structure up ahead. There are trees near the opening which will provide shelter from the rain and cold wind.

They followed the scout back to the location and Erik

agreed it was a fortunate find. They dismounted, some men taking the horses to be fed, while others sought what dry kindling they could find to start a fire.

Not soon after, a large fire provided warmth for both the men and horses. They hung cloaks, bed rolls and other items close to the fire to dry whilst standing closer in an effort to warm themselves.

Torac neared. "Hopefully it will not be too long of a ride to our destination. I want to see what has been done by the guards who came ahead of us. They should have our guard-house and stables built by now."

"Aye, I hope so. Although Laird Ross has not heard from them in over a fortnight." He shook his head. "They were never the most reliable, which was why they were sent here and not to battle in the north with us."

"They are disappointments then," Torac said. Looking into the fire he changed the subject. "I hope we can rest tonight. Tomorrow will be a long day."

The limp wet blankets showed no sign of drying, and with the continued rainfall, Erik doubted they would be usable. "We will have to gather branches and build elevated beds for the night. No use in dawdling."

Once ordered, the men collected long branches and stacked them, each making their own bed. Some slept in the cave, others closer to the fire. Erik opted for the fire, as he detested closed-in spaces. It was a fear he'd never outgrown.

As a child he'd become lost in a cave once. It had been a nightmare. The more he walked the darker it had become until he could not see his own hand before his face. He'd crouched down and cried, his teeth chattering with fear. Thick blobs of wetness had plopped down on him, each time making him shudder in terror.

At the sight of a torch, he'd screamed for help. His father had lifted him from the wet ground and carried him out. It was then he'd seen all the bats hanging over him. It was an experience he'd never forgotten or gotten over apparently. Just looking toward the cave made his skin crawl.

"A hot meal will make it all better." Auley MacBain, the cook, hurried from the creek with a large pot of water and hung it over the fire using an iron stand they'd brought. He then began chopping onions.

"What are we eating?" Erik asked. "Onion soup?"

"Nay, they've caught three fish already. A few more and we'll have a hearty stew," the ruddy, red-haired Scot replied in his usual brisk tone.

It had been a long time since Erik had eaten fish stew and his mouth watered in expectation. Instead of standing there and watching Auley cook, he went to check on his cloak. Surprisingly, it was drying. He flipped it so the other side would face the fire.

Balgair, another warrior, came closer. "How far will we be from Creag?"

The warrior was blood thirsty, the type of man every fighter wanted on his side. Erik hoped they'd be visible to the village of Creag. "We will be next to the forest that divides our lands.

"Good. The sooner we deal with them the better."

"We will start patrols immediately upon arriving."

"There are reports of archers in the trees," Torac said walking toward them.

"We shall send archers with each patrol. Two will go with each set of warriors. Once Struan arrives, he makes five." Erik let out a breath, his mind going over all that had to be done in a short time.

Torac let out a harsh breath. "Aye that is a good idea."

It was good to have Torac with him. Along with their friend Struan, the three of them had fought together often and had developed a strong friendship.

Erik relied heavily on Torac for advice as the warrior was well versed on warfare and patrols. "Once we arrive in the morning, we can decide what is best upon assessing the situation."

Torac walked away and went to sit with a group of others who had completed their tasks. The man remained silent, his gaze on the fire that now burned bright.

Torac was as capable as Erik was, if not more so. In the years of knowing him, Erik had never seen him lose his temper. It did not make him weak; on the contrary, there was a silent strength about him that was as fearsome as any shout or strike.

Upon laying down for the night, Erik could not sleep, his mind whirling over what needed to be done and hoping to make the right decisions.

The air had a salty smell that reminded him of his youth on the Isle of Skye. His family home was near the shore, and he'd spent many days fishing and swimming.

As a warrior, he'd fought for the laird and had constantly moved from one place to the other, not settling anywhere long. In a way, the keep was as close a home as he had. It was where his belongings had remained in a small room in the guard quarters.

He'd emptied the room upon receiving the assignment of coming to the southwestern corner of the isle, where he'd remain for months. Perhaps he would settle there, in Welland.

The lonesome hoots of an owl brought his mind to the present. Erik turned to his side and attempted to get comfortable.

Still unable to settle his mind, he considered all the responsibilities that were on his shoulders. He had to make certain he thought things through before making any decisions. Tomorrow they would arrive to set up in an area they were not very familiar with. Whatever awaited would have to be dealt with.

IT WAS A miserable night. No one got much sleep as the rainfall seeped through every opening between branches. Everyone and everything was completely soaked by morning.

When the sun finally rose, it was barely visible through thick gray clouds. The mist rising from the ground made for quite a dreary beginning to the day.

"Let us divert and go to the village to eat," Erik said. "At least there we can find a tavern to get out of the elements for a bit and warm our bones."

At the prospect of a hot meal, the men were more than happy to pack their soggy things and mount.

They rode in silence two by two toward the larger village. The promise of a hot meal and warm shelter helped them put up with the gloomy weather.

To Erik's annoyance, it began to rain harder. It was doubtful any of the attackers would be out that day, which was the only thing he could feel good about at the moment. Drenched through and the wind blowing from the nearby sea made for a miserable journey.

By the time they arrived at Welland, the rain had dwindled to a drizzle and villagers hurried out to greet them. Children waved with wide grins while adults were a bit more tentative in their welcome.

They slowed when arriving at the village square where a gray-haired man waited, with an eager expression, for Erik and Torac to dismount before approaching. "Welcome to Welland, I am Athol, the constable"—he motioned to the woman with him—"and this is my wife, Helene."

Erik nodded to the woman before addressing the man. "I am Erik, and he is called Torac, we come at the laird's request to see about restoring peace to the area."

"I have gone several times to see him to ask for help. It is good to see I was heard," Athol replied, a grin spitting his face.

There was no need to tell the man about all the other issues in the northern portion of the island that required attention and that was why it had taken them so long to come see about them. The man had to stand by and watch as his people were attacked and had done his best to defend his small village. He did not need to hear excuses.

"We will seek to ensure yer people remain safe," Torac said. "Who, besides the men we sent ahead, are here to help defend?"

The man looked toward the south. By the lack of expression, it was obvious he was not at all impressed by the guards who'd been sent by the laird months earlier. It was only a small contingent of four, but it was all that could be spared.

"They seem to spend most of the time chasing after lasses and expecting to be fed," Athol said. "Although grateful for their presence, they did not escort a group that traveled to the shore to seek passage on birlinns to visit kinfolk and the people ended up being attacked."

The man shook his head. "I am sorry to not speak well of my laird's men. Besides them, we have a small group of men who are learning to fight. However it is hard to defend against archers."

"The truth is appreciated," Erik said. "Is there a place for my men and I to warm up and have a good meal?"

They went to the village tavern. Inside there were plenty of tables and chairs and to their delight, a large fireplace that warmed the room through. Cloaks were draped over chairs that were dragged closer to the fire to help dry them.

The tavern owner and his helpers quickly dispatched ale, bread, and freshly churned butter. After a few minutes, bowls of hearty stew were slid before them along with offerings of cheese.

People lingered near the long table, some drinking ale, while others looked on with interest.

"Ye have been kind to serve us so quickly," Erik told the tavern owner. "It is much appreciated."

The man gawked when Erik paid him more than enough to cover the food and drink. "Thank ye."

Torac spoke to the constable, who gave them shortcut directions to where their post would be. Once again, it was clear the guards assigned there had not come to the village often, and the constable was not aware of any patrols.

Erik's blood boiled. The guards who'd been sent ahead had not taken their orders seriously.

If they'd been patrolling as expected, they would have known a large contingent of armed warriors had entered the village and would soon head their way.

"Make arrangements with the constable and ensure he is paid enough coin to procure our meals over the next few days," Erik told Torac, who walked off to do as told.

BY THE TIME they rode up to the camp, Erik was enraged. The area was silent. Barks from inside the guardhouse meant a dog was kept inside. Other than four horses in the stables, there were no signs of the guards assigned there.

He jumped from his horse, drew his sword, and raced into the building with several warriors close behind.

Sleeping men awoke with a start and practically fell from their cots at the commotion. The only thing standing up to the intrusion was a hound who bared his teeth and growled.

Erik looked to the dog. "Good hound." He made a hand signal to the dog, and it wagged its tail in recognition. Seeming smarter than the four idiots who scrambled to stand, the hound rounded the newcomers and loped outside.

The groggy guardsmen didn't try to get to their swords as they were by the doorway, which meant they would have to go past Erik and his men.

On one of the cots a woman sat ramrod still, not bothering to cover her nakedness, her mouth agape and hair askew.

"Get dressed and get out," Erik gritted out each word.

The woman slid from the cot, picked up her discarded clothes, and ran out, not bothering to dress.

Erik walked closer to the guardsmen. "Is this how ye perform yer duties?" he yelled. "Is this how ye represent our laird?"

One of the men managed a sheepish look. "We usually are on patrol…"

"Line up!" Erik yelled, interrupting him. "Now!"

The four hapless idiots stood shoulder to shoulder, none fully dressed.

Erik met each of their gazes. "None of ye were aware that I and a contingent of twenty rode into the center of the village. We could have decimated the entirety of them by now."

Realizing they had no excuse all four looked to the ground. The same one who'd spoken before met his gaze and then away. "I accept that we have failed in our duties. We are only four…"

"When was the last time ye escorted people to the shoreline?"

No reply.

"When was the last time ye scouted the forest?"

Again there was silence.

"Go outside and remain standing. I require time to decide how best to proceed."

Two men, who'd obviously been enjoying the woman's company, grabbed their clothes and hurried out behind the other two, who were already half dressed.

Eric walked around the large interior noting with disgust the rotting food atop the tables and the fact none of the tasks the men had been assigned had been completed.

They were supposed to have built cots and fortified the stables. Additionally, the men had been instructed to set up regular visits by villagers to bring food and to help with construction, in exchange for payment.

Obviously the men had spent the money in other ways, expecting the warriors not to arrive for another few months.

He was glad for Darach's discretion in not sending word ahead. The laird must have suspected what had occurred.

Torac ordered men to sweep out spaces for the horses in the dilapidated stable. Then they brought water and fresh feed. The feed troughs had been kept filled, so at least the four had been caring well for their horses.

The dirty tables were dragged outside and some of the men made several trips to the nearby creek to bring back water to scrub them clean.

A few minutes later several villagers came to help them set up. The people were glad for their arrival.

Torac's flat gaze met Erik's then turned to the four men, who stood in a line waiting to hear what their punishment would be. "The villagers said they only paid once for food, the rest of the time they demanded it. They've never spent a coin for anything else."

"I believe they spent coin, but not for what was directed by the laird," Erik replied.

"Tie them to a tree each," Torac directed to his men. "Facing the tree."

Two of the four tried to escape but were quickly caught. All four struggled to get free as they were dragged toward the trees.

"I will see to the punishment," Torac said. "Two of them are mine. The other two Struan's."

Erik walked away and went into the stables. The anger

boiled over once again when noting the idiots had not bothered to chop any firewood. There was no stockpile set aside and they all needed to dry their soaked belongings.

Ignoring the shivering, he went back out and found that some men were already chopping wood. Hopefully, it would be dry enough to burn without filling the storehouse with smoke.

The fates decided to be kind and the sun peeked out from between the clouds while he and several men carried wood into the guardhouse.

After two trips, he started a fire in the hearth that quickly dispelled the dampness in the room.

They would be sleeping on the damp bedding that night since it would be impossible to dry all of it by the fire.

"Start a bonfire outside," Erik instructed. "Set up racks to dry some of the bedding."

"It is being done," a guard replied.

Auley, entered the room, his mouth curled into a snarl. "What am I supposed to do with this?" He motioned to the fireplace. "With all the tartans about, I cannot cook. They won't let me near the bonfire outside, say it's to dry the rest of the bedding."

"Meals will be brought today," Erik replied. "I was told there is an area that was used as a kitchen before."

Without a word, Auley turned on his heel and stalked out.

There was much to do, but first he had to ensure the men were aware of their duties.

Outside, Auley and a young lad from the village carried rocks and were building something under the cover of a tilting structure. Each place he looked made Erik angrier at the four who'd been there for several months. So much should have been accomplished.

He whistled to get everyone's attention and the men stopped what they were doing and came to stand before him.

Torac walked up and gave him a quizzical look. "Our first assignment will now be to set up our area," he muttered under his breath.

"I want to kill the idiots," Erik snapped. He looked to the men gathered. "The carpenters from the village will assist in building cots and tables and help to set up the kitchen for Auley."

Erik pointed to the side. "There is a shack on the side there where Torac, Balgair, and I will sleep, as there isn't enough room for everyone in the guardhouse."

"The cots will be done by nightfall," one of the men volunteered.

There were murmurs of how they'd have beds, but no bedding, some of the men laughed.

"Patrols will begin on the morrow. Instructions will be given at first meal."

Torac gave him an annoyed look as the men went off to continue their tasks.

"Ye have something to say, ye should say it," Erik said once the men were gone.

After an exhalation of breath, Torac turned to him. "If we are to work well together, we should discuss what will be said to the men prior to ye doing it."

"I am the lead…"

"I am well aware of what ye are," Torac replied, his nostril flaring. "Half of them are my men, and they will receive orders from me if I am to lead them properly."

Erik couldn't see how that mattered right then as everyone was mostly setting up the area.

"And all of them are my men, including ye," he retorted, unable to keep from raising his voice.

When Torac turned away, Erik stormed off. It was no use speaking to the stubborn silent man.

Several wooden frames had been built next to the large bonfire upon which tartans were draped to hopefully dry out before nightfall.

The four who'd been whipped under Torac's instructions sat limply tied to the trees. Eric realized he was unaware of how many lashings they'd received. He looked toward where Torac had returned to work and decided not to ask.

Just then a young lad hurried from the direction of the village and made a beeline for him. "Sir, the women come with food. They request ye ensure they are not bothered upon nearing."

"I will ensure it." Erik looked to the men tied to the trees and motioned so the young lad could see. "They will not bother the women of the village again."

The lad's eyes widened, and his mouth formed an "O" before he raced to inform the women who came to feed them.

Upon arriving he'd not been aware of having to make peace with two sets of people, not just the enemy, but those of his own clan as well.

HE DIDN'T WANT to eat, not then. Once the men ate, he'd eat whatever was left. The four men had to be punished and sent back to the keep. It was either that or keep them there and have to continuously keep an eye on them. He'd leave the decision to Torac.

Needing to clear his head, he walked to the woods' edge and looked up to the treetops. The foliage was quite dense, which meant they'd have to go slowly on horseback.

Erik was considering if they should go on foot when the faintest rustling sound caught his attention. He didn't turn toward the sound, so not to let whoever was there know he'd heard.

Going to a tree, he pulled down the front of his breeches and relieved himself, the entire time keeping a keen ear.

A twig snapped and then there was silence. Out of the corner of his eye, he caught the slightest movement. Whomever it was had a slight build, like that of a young lad or a woman.

Springing to action, he rushed toward the figure grabbing them from behind as the person turned to flee.

"Release me at once," the woman demanded in a low tone. It was curious that she did not scream. Instead, she struggled, kicking and wiggling as if possessed.

"I will if ye stop fighting me," Erik said.

When she calmed, he released his hold and pulled her around to face him. The streaks of dirt across her cheeks and disheveled hair did not distract from her beauty. She had dark auburn hair and the darkest brown eyes he'd ever seen.

Her full lips were twisted into a sneer, and she glared at him. "Can a person not walk through the forest freely?" she asked. "Is it against the laws of yer people?"

"Ye were skulking about," Erik replied. "Spying."

She grunted and rolled her eyes. "Why would I do that?"

"Ye tell me."

Just then a young lad appeared through the trees. "Come, Esme, we must go," he said softly. When the lad met his gaze, he didn't seem at all intimidated. "Release my sister at once."

"Where do ye live?" Erik asked. He'd yet to release her arm.

The woman looked past his shoulder. Obviously some of his men had come to see what happened.

When Erik turned to look, a sharp pain between his legs made him drop to the ground. As his vision blurred, he grabbed the affected area with both hands.

The woman and the lad dashed away through the trees, quick as hares.

If not for his inability to speak, he would have ordered his men to give chase. Finally, Torac instructed a pair of men to follow, but to be at a distance in case the woman had been sent to draw them out.

"Can ye stand?" Torac asked. Upon Erik nodding Torac grabbed his hand and pulled him to his feet.

"Women cause us to let our guard down," Torac said in a flat voice. "That is why I do not trust nary of them."

Erik let out a breath, thankfully the pain was receding. "I must agree with ye in this instance."

The men returned and reported the pair had gone across the creek to the village responsible for the attacks.

"Spying for coin," Torac murmured. "They send young lads and women in hopes they will not be suspected."

CHAPTER TWO

THREE DAYS LATER, Esme ran her hands down her arms in an effort to warm herself. It was useless of course as she'd been shivering for the last hour barely able to keep her teeth from chattering. She pushed branches out of the way and peered through them to watch the men working. By their build and dress, they were warriors. Since arriving they'd been fortifying a structure and working on stables. It seemed they planned to remain indefinitely.

Trees were chopped down and piles of firewood were carried toward the large storehouse where, up until recently only four guardsmen had been living.

The lazy four—as she'd been calling them—who rarely did more than walk around the building, were nowhere in sight. Often she'd seen them leaving in the direction of the village or returning with a woman in tow.

Next to the building was a man that stood out from the rest. Unlike most Scotsmen, his hair, which fell in waves to his shoulders, was the color of sunrays. He was the one who'd caught her a few days earlier. Although from this distance she could not see them, she knew his eyes were the most curious color, somewhere between gray and light blue.

Built like a warrior, he seemed to be the one in charge by the way he walked from group to group and spoke, seeming to give orders.

The blond man went over to a huge muscular man and by their expressions and the way the blond man stalked away, they looked to have argued.

As she scanned the scene before her, she counted the men and horses, then calculated what she'd report when returning to her village.

Having grown up as a foundling along with her younger brother, Laith, they'd become adept at finding ways to earn coin to feed themselves.

Learning of her ability to move about silently and knowing that being a lass she'd not be suspected of spying, the village council had sent her regularly to do just that—spy on the camp.

Several days earlier, when she'd been caught by the blond man, she'd come to see what the lazy four were doing and had stumbled upon a goldmine. With the information about the large group of warriors, the council would surely reward her with enough coin to be able to purchase flour and meat.

However, she would have to be smart about it. About how much information to dole out to them. If she informed them of everything, they would only pay her once. However, if she spaced it out, they would pay her several times.

She doubted anyone else from her village knew about their arrivals. A group of men from her village stalked travelers, though they rarely ventured this far. Instead, the cowards robbed those who ventured too close to their territory.

Although aware of the robbers, the council looked the other way, using the excuse of keeping trespassers and the possibility of danger away from the village as a reason for not punishing the thieves.

Esme knew better, what the council did was keep outsiders away who would threaten their control over the people.

Her village was a mixture of good and evil. Neither seeming to outbalance the other. On one hand, they were a sturdy lot who took care of each other. On the other, the council oversaw everything maintaining strict and often unfair control.

Too cold to remain longer, Esme decided to return home. As she headed toward her cottage on the outskirts of the village, she considered what she'd report. Perhaps she'd tell them she'd seen horsemen headed toward Welland and give an inaccurate count. Then she'd volunteer to return and see what they were about.

They would probably send someone with her, though she hoped not as she didn't trust any man who worked for the council.

Earlier the blond man had barked out orders and she'd overheard him say that half of the men would patrol the villages and farms. At least if they did send someone with her, they would only see half of the guardsmen.

At her stomach's insistence for food, she could not remain longer, and Esme slipped silently into the foliage and hurried down the path she kept clear to ensure her passage lacked sound. Upon emerging from the woods, she was free to again walk in the open.

A while later, she entered a small cottage carrying a pair of fish an older man from the village had given her in exchange for helping him gather firewood.

Inside the cottage, an elderly woman sat in front of the fire, her closed eyes disappearing in the wrinkles of her face.

Laith, who was ten and three sat up from his position on the floor. "Ye caught fish?"

"No," Esme replied with a smile. "Old man Hamish gave them to us."

She went to the hearth and warmed her hands. "I am chilled to the bone. I must put on dry clothes at once."

The old woman opened her eyes. "Ye are here at last. I require food." The words were barely audible.

Esme neared and patted the woman's frail shoulder. "Today we will have a feast of fish and carrots."

The woman smiled displaying a lack of teeth.

No one knew how old Mege was. She'd already been of advanced age when she'd taken in Esme and Laith. Esme had been a wee girl of about nine with a toddler in tow when they'd appeared cold and hungry, walking from the forest.

Esme long suspected their parents had been attacked and probably killed by the same men who continued to attack innocent travelers. So many years later, as much as she wished to know the truth, with the daily struggle to earn coin or food, she had little time to ponder it. She'd given up questioning Mege, who insisted the fae had brought them from the forest as a gift to her.

"I see ye have been busy as well," Esme told Laith, who beamed in response.

"Aye, I helped clean out pens and weeded a garden for Ian. He paid me and gifted me carrots."

Esme's eyes became moist at seeing the two coins he'd left on the table. Her brother must have worked all day to earn it. "We should have enough saved up to purchase fabric for a new tunic for ye."

While the stew boiled, she busied herself making dough for flatbread as they'd no yeast for making baked bread. Nonetheless, it would be a good meal.

They owned a goat, four laying hens, and a rooster. Along with milk and eggs for Mege, who loved them, they always had just enough to sustain them.

Esme dreamed of a larger cottage, of new dresses and shoes, but they could rarely afford one garment a year for her and Mege. She ensured her brother had better clothes; thick fabrics that would keep him warm as he often worked out in the weather.

Once Mege was fed and helped into the bed, Esme and Laith sat at the table. The candlelight gave the small space a warm glow.

"Tomorrow, I am working with Hamish," Laith said. "He asked me to help him mend the pens for winter. I will have steady work for a few days. Ye do not have to worry."

Esme frowned. "It is good to hear. One of us has to keep an eye on her." She looked to the bed where Mege was wheezing. "She is unwell."

"Aye."

THE NEXT DAY, Esme waited until the old woman was napping and slipped out. The council rarely met until late in the day and usually only a few times a month. In her opinion, they did little else than torment people with their rules and punishments. All the while claiming to be keeping the peace and ensuring the people of the village were safe.

Hers was a remote village called Creag, on the southwestern corner of the isle of North Uist. Being situated between the sea, the mountains, and the forest, they rarely had travelers come through.

A majority of the villagers were born, lived, and died there in Creag, never seeming to see a need to leave. Other than the occasional peddler, who managed to get past the men in the forest, they rarely saw any outsiders.

Carrying baskets she'd woven and hoped to sell, Esme stopped upon seeing one of the councilmen's sons.

A shiver of warning crawled up her spine and she decided it was best to avoid the burly man. He was called Tavon and was forever tormenting her.

"Oy, Esme. Come here lass," he called out.

Turning to him, Esme assumed a calm demeanor despite her heart hammering in her chest.

"What is it?" She'd neared, ensuring to keep as much distance as possible.

"Where are ye going?"

She lifted the baskets. "To the square."

"I'll buy one. Come here."

There was little she could do. A glance over her shoulder made her even more unsettled. There was no one about.

"That would be kind of ye," she managed. "Which one?"

His narrowed eyes scanned over her. "Come close so I can inspect them better."

When she hesitated, he closed the distance between them, grabbed her hair, and yanked her to the side of the cottage where he lived.

"Are ye scared of me Esme?" His breath fanned over her face, as she winced in pain. Still she clung to the baskets, as if it would help.

"Answer me."

"I am a bit, yes." She told him what he wanted to hear. In truth more than anything she abhorred the man. Wished him dead. "Let me go, it hurts."

His lips curved and he pushed himself against her until she could barely breathe. "Do ye remember our time together?" he asked, his mouth to her ear. "To me it was not memorable, but nonetheless if ye wish, we can be together again."

The bastard spoke as if she'd had any choice in the matter. "I would like to go to the square now," Esme managed. "Please."

When Tavon chuckled, it was without mirth. "Aye, well, I have things to do. But I will come to ye soon."

Slowly he pushed off of her. It was only then she noted several people had appeared and looked on with interest. When he looked over at them, they shuffled away, not one daring to come to her rescue.

On the contrary, one of the women looked at her with disdain. The largest basket fell from her hand, and she winced when Tavon stomped on it.

He tossed a coin at her chest. It bounced and landed on the ground. "For the wee basket."

The last thing she wanted was to pick up the coin but thinking of how much it would help if she could save up to purchase necessities, she grabbed it and hurried to the market.

"What happened to yer hair?" Lattie, a young woman with a babe on her hip looked her over. "Ye look as if ye've just had a fright." She motioned to the side of her table where she displayed pots she and her husband made from clay. "Ye can put yer baskets there."

Esme carefully arranged the baskets, placing the wildflowers she'd collected—though now a bit wilted—inside several of them to hopefully entice people to buy them. She then loosened her hair and braided it.

"Tavon again," she whispered to Lattie.

"Ye should tell his father," her friend said with a frown.

Esme shrugged. "I do not know what to do. No one believed me when he forced himself on me and I complained to the council."

"He is a ripe bastard." Lattie shifted her bairn to the other hip. "Try yer best to keep away from him else ye'll be carrying his bairn and be stuck with 'im."

The thought made Esme shiver. She'd been terrified of being with child the last time he'd forced himself on her. Thankfully, it had not happened. She'd followed Mege's instructions to bath in the creek right after and drink a foul-tasting tea the old woman had concocted.

"I want to leave and never return." Esme told her friend. "Poor Laith is working too hard for his age. People only give him tasks no one else wishes to do, Other than yer husband, Ian, who spend time with him and teaches him about farming."

Lattie gave her a worried look. "If ye leave, then who will look after Mege? She will die if left alone."

At the old woman's name, Esme realized she could not linger much longer. "I have to return home soon. Can I leave the baskets with ye?"

"Aye," Lattie said. "First let us share a meal." She handed Esme the bairn, who proceeded to suck his thumb and lay his head on her shoulder. The boy was as sweet as his mother.

Lattie pulled a cloth back from the basket she'd purchased months before from Esme, inside were bread, cheese, and a pair of apples.

They ate while Lattie talked about her husband's mother who was recently widowed and had moved in with them. "It is quite the adjustment," Lattie explained. "I do not know how to be around her. She is so sad."

"It must be heartbreaking to lose one's husband after so many years of marriage," Esme replied.

Just then, a woman approached and purchased two small pots and one of Esme's baskets. The woman's companion lifted a particularly intricate one and looked to Esme.

"Ye should concentrate on making baskets. These are very well made."

"Thank ye," Esme replied. "I plan to make more like that one."

The woman handed her a coin. "It is better to earn money with our hands than with our bodies."

Her stomach turned and the food she'd just eaten threatened to come back up. Esme could only stare at the women as they walked away talking loudly enough for her to hear about how some women could not seem to keep from being whores.

"They're bitter old shrews. Do not pay them any heed. Everyone knows Tavon and his ilk force themselves on unprotected lasses. Ye and the others who have complained have never been listened to. It is only because his father is an elder in the council, so Tavon gets away with it."

"His father is no better," Esme said wiping away a tear. "I best go."

On the way home Esme realized she'd not told anyone about the warriors at the camp. Perhaps it was best to keep the secret for now.

She shuddered to think what would happen if Tavon dared to come to her cottage and Laith was there. Her brother was no match for the bulkier man.

The Clan Ross warriors were there for a reason. Probably to see about the attacks on their people by hers. If that was the case, would they protect someone who brought them information?

Was it possible that the blond leader might help her escape from the possibility of being taken by Tavon and left with child this time?

Her mind awhirl, she didn't notice that someone followed her home.

A rock hit her between the shoulders, and she flinched. When she turned, two young boys threw another rock then raced away to pick up more stones.

"Whore! Whore!" the two lads called out laughing.

Dodging the stones, Esme hurried into her cottage, the boys finally giving up and running away.

Thankfully Mege was still sound asleep when she entered the cottage. The reprieve gave her time to run a damp cloth over her face and inspect where she could for bruising. It would not do for Laith to see them.

Although young and slight, he always did his best to protect her.

"Wake up sweet lady," Esme cooed helping the old woman to sit. "How about some milky porridge?"

Mege shook her head. "I am not hungry at all."

It was worrisome that the old woman ate less and less each day. "I will sweeten it with honey," Esme said with a smile. "Ye like that."

Mege's eyes widened. "Honey?"

"Aye, but ye must get up first."

It took several tries and more convincing before she was able to get Mege up, washed, and sitting in her favorite chair. It was by the front door where she could look out at the small garden they'd planted together.

After carefully measuring out the bit of honey that she kept in a clay pot gifted to them by Lattie, she handed the bowl to Mege to drink from. Carefully she helped the old woman to bring it to her lips.

It was late by the time Laith arrived, looking haggard. He carried a cabbage and some skinny carrots in the sack that she'd packed food for him in that morning. "Hamish insisted I bring these and asked if ye could go by tomorrow and pluck a chicken for his pot."

The old man couldn't do much with his gnarled fingers. It was astounding that he somehow managed to grow a lush vegetable garden.

"Is his wife not there?" Esme asked as she slid a plate of food in front of her exhausted brother.

"Aye, she is, but says she cannot see well enough to do it properly."

Esme sat down and met her brother's gaze. "We should consider leaving this place, Laith. We should go far from here. Surely, there is a better life elsewhere."

"How?" Laith looked to where Mege once again slept. "We cannot travel with her. She is too weak."

It took a moment for her to form the words and she whispered. "She is not long for this world. After…"

Laith nodded. "If ye wish, I will go with ye. But if we are caught."

"What do they care if we decide to leave? We live in a village, not a prison."

Both knew the council would want to know why they wished to leave and would not look upon it kindly. Those who had left had always done so under the cover of darkness. Otherwise, they made up excuses of visiting family. It meant they would have to leave everything behind, not wishing to draw suspicion that they did not plan to return.

Looking about the cottage, the dismal space would not be hard to leave. They owned little of any value.

"I heard about Tavon. Is that why?" Laith met her gaze, a hardness in his expression. "Did he… hurt ye?"

Esme shook her head. "Nay. Do not worry. I can take care of myself."

When her brother yawned widely, she covered his hand with hers. "Rest Laith, ye have to get up early."

Moments later, he slept soundly on his cot by the fireplace.

It didn't matter how much she asked, he refused to sleep on the more comfortable bed. Leaving it for her and Mege to share.

Laith would grow up to be a good man. But now more than ever, Esme was convinced they had to leave.

Given the opportunity, he could work for the laird and earn more without having to work so hard.

As she climbed into bed, Esme considered that perhaps the sooner she approached the blond warrior and asked him to help, the better.

CHAPTER THREE

WHEN HIS STEED'S demeanor suddenly changed, Erik signaled for the others to stop. On patrol for the second time in a sennight, he was beginning to learn the portion of the forest closest to Welland.

They had not ventured much further until that day, making them extra cautious of every stirring, sound, and change in their horses.

A wild boar snorted as it hurried from sight, the usually fierce protector of their territory had obviously considered the four war horses too big an adversary.

"Three more," one of his men said pointing toward the undergrowth and sure enough a sow with a pair of piglets hurried after the first one.

"Would have made a good meal," Erik murmured, annoyed that they could not take the time to hunt as they had to remain as quiet as possible in case enemy archers were nearby.

After searching the surrounding trees, the warrior in front gave a signal and they continued further south, following directions the scouts had given.

A bubbling creek wound through the woods, the steady gurgling sounds of running water giving the area they rode through a peaceful sense. Birdsong competed with the sounds of the creek and the occasional lonely call of a wolf.

As they neared the water, the birds went silent, no doubt watching them from high in the trees.

His men spread in a line, each one carefully scanning the trees and surrounding foliage. "Nothing so far," Balgair, a brusque warrior, who seemed to prefer battle over peace grumbled.

"Perhaps they are aware we are here and large in number," Erik replied. "It has been too peaceful as of late."

At the sound of voices, they exchanged looks. Erik motioned for two men to remain, while he and Balgair dismounted.

Minding where they stepped, he and the warrior quietly crept toward the sounds, bent forward so as not to be seen above some of the bushes.

A young woman sunk her bucket into the water and looked on as an older one did the same.

"It is not safe to venture so far from yer cottage," the young one scolded. "Why do ye insist on creek water?"

She took the bucket from the older woman and headed away. Erik studied the young woman. She seemed familiar, perhaps she was the woman he'd caught upon first arriving.

He assumed the older woman was either her or her husband's mother.

In the distance was a cottage where an old man stood holding a dead chicken and looking out toward the women. He'd built a fire, no doubt over which the bird would be prepared.

When the women neared, the old man presented the younger one with the chicken and they went into the cottage.

"Nothing of interest," Balgair said. "I doubt they have anything to do with the attacks."

"It depends on who her husband is. They are closest to the edge of the forest, which means this would be a perfect place to gather and plan the attacks."

"Aye, true." Balgair stared at the cottage. "There is nowt we can do but keep watch."

They returned to the horses and mounted. Traveling along the edge of the woods they headed toward the sea. As they neared the area where some of the attacks had taken place, once again they stopped and listened intently for any unusual sounds.

If the attackers were smart, they had been alerted to the presence of others by the silencing of the birds.

Moments later, an arrow flew from the treetops, narrowly missing one of the men. They held up their shields so that the archer among them could take aim. Unfortunately, it was impossible to see where the man hid.

No one came through the trees to attack. It meant whoever they were had sized them up and realized they'd be unable to win against a group of seasoned warriors.

"There," Balgair whispered pointing up. The archer took aim and moments later, a man fell from the tree, landing with a solid thump.

"Ah!" the man yelled, while rolling side to side. With an arrow impaled in his upper arm and the high probability he twisted his foot upon hitting the ground, it was clear the man was in a great deal of pain.

Remaining vigilant, two warriors approached the moaning man, while the rest of them kept watch.

"Why did ye shoot at us?" one of Erik's men asked the howling man.

"I-I am d-defending p-people." The man finally managed to get out.

Who's land they were on was hard to tell. As far as Erik knew most of the isle belonged to Clan Ross. Only the small southwest corner had been claimed by a Macdonald, who as far as he knew died many years before.

"I am not sure to believe ye," Erik said to the man, who seemed on the brink of passing out.

"Help me." The man began moaning anew.

Erik led his horse closer. "Not if we are to be attacked."

"Old Hamish's cottage. No—no one of threat is there." The man motioned toward the area they'd just come from. "Pl-please," he whispered before unconsciousness took him.

"Fine." Erik motioned to two men, who lifted the man who remained silent and limp. They retraced their route and with an archer at his back and the other warriors spread out, Erik approached the cottage where the women had gone.

At seeing them, the young woman straightened from her task of plucking the bird. With a chicken in one hand, the young woman lifted the other and covered her mouth. He immediately recognized her as the lass who'd kicked him. Esme.

"Do ye know this man?" Erik asked meeting her gaze.

The dark heavily lashed pools seemed to send a message. She looked over her shoulder to the interior. "Ye are Clan Ross are ye not?"

"Aye." Erik looked over to the warrior who had the injured man over the horse. "We bring ye a man who shot at us from a tree. He is injured and asked to be brought here. Do ye recognize him?"

"I do." She looked at the man for only an instant, giving Erik the impression she did not care for him.

"Perhaps summon yer husband to come and retrieve him."

"I do not…" She hesitated. "The only one here is Hamish, he is an old man. He is too feeble to help."

Erik motioned for his other men to move closer. They pulled the injured man from the horse and carried him to the front of the cottage depositing him on the ground.

At this point, the old man—who he assumed was Hamish—and his wife hurried out. The old man looked him up and down.

"Ah, so warriors have come." He smiled widely and then looked to the injured man. "What happened to Tavon?"

"He fell from a tree," the young woman replied dryly. "They brought him to be nursed."

The old man neared and touched the injured man with the toe of his foot. "Tavon. Are ye alive?"

The injured man moaned.

"Ah, he will recover." The old man met Erik's gaze. "Troublemakers the lot of them. Get what they deserve."

Taking the plucked chicken, the old man gave the young woman a tap on her shoulder. "Thank ye, Esme, ye and yer brother help us so much. Go on home now. Rest."

The lass looked to Erik. "Why are ye here?"

"Seeing after our people who are being attacked by yers. We wish to know why."

She slid a look to the injured man who was demanding the old man go and fetch his brother. "Ye should leave. The men from the village are not kind to newcomers."

"Who leads them?"

"Stop talking to them, whore, and go fetch my brothers!" The injured man managed.

At his words, her wide eyes met Erik's for a second before she turned and hurried away with her head bent and her shawl pulled tight around her shoulders.

"Ye all should get away from our lands." The man was regaining his strength if how loudly he was now speaking was anything to go by.

Erik figured whoever was in the forest with him was collecting men to come and fight.

"We should go," Balgair said.

"Tell yer constable, we wish to meet with them," Erik said looking at the old man, who nodded.

In the distance they spotted a large group of horsemen. Erik mounted, then he and his men galloped away to the forest and back the way they'd come.

Thankfully, he remembered the quickest way back and as soon as they crossed the creek, those in pursuit stopped following them.

"They are well aware of how far to go," Erik told Balgair, who grunted in response.

ERIK RELATED WHAT happened to Torac, as he and his men were about to go on night patrol. During the night, they did not venture into the forest, instead, they kept to the areas that belonged to Clan Ross.

The area they were responsible for was vast. Encompassing Welland, the smaller village of Aldness, and a farming community of dwellings, fields, and herds of sheep. It would be hard to ensure everyone's safety with them only being able to use ten men at a time. However, the laird did not deem it possible to spare more.

Erik walked from the guardhouse to the kitchen area where Auley stirred something in a boiling pot. The man grumbled at his helper to hurry and fetch water. The young lad raced away after giving Erik a glance that told him he was holding his tongue.

"One day the lad is going to strangle ye in yer sleep," Erik said with a chuckle.

"He would not dare," Auley retorted. "Did ye make it to the village?"

"To the edge, aye. As expected, they are not a friendly lot."

The cook grunted. "Idiots."

It was true. If Laird Ross decided to, they could overtake the village easily. Instead, the laird was patient, standing by the treaty that had been agreed to by one of his predecessors.

"True. I saw a lass plucking a bird and thought how it has been a long time since I've had chicken for a meal."

"What did the lass look like?" Auley asked with a raised eyebrow. "Perhaps it is a lass that ye have not had for a while."

Erik could not help but laugh. The man had a quick wit. "That is also true."

THE NEXT AFTERNOON, Erik became restless. It was not his turn to patrol, therefore, he had little to do.

Men were assigned to build a smaller guardhouse, which would give Erik, Torac, and Struan—when he arrived—a place to sleep that was away from the lower ranks. Erik offered to help, but they insisted they had a plan in place and did not require his assistance.

He mounted and guided his horse to the creek deciding to go for a swim. Moments later as his horse nibbled on the green grasses, he swam in the frigid water.

The horse's head popped up and immediately Erik sunk down into the water with only his eyes above it. Someone was spying on him.

"May I speak to ye?"

It was the young lass who'd been at the cottage earlier. "'Tis important."

He looked past her and then around and up to the trees before wading to the bank where his clothes were.

"Wait," Erik instructed.

The entire time he dressed both he and she kept an eye on one another. Neither trusting the other fully.

Finally, he mounted and directed his horse across the water to where she stood and then dismounted.

"What is it?"

She looked up at him for a long moment seeming to reconsider. It gave him the opportunity to study her. Just as he recalled, she was quite lovely. Her eyes were almond shaped and her lips plump. Although her faded clothes seemed to indicate she was very poor, the way she stood, and her graceful movements gave the impression of high birth.

"Are ye a Macdonald?" Erik asked.

She shrugged. "I do not know my surname. My brother and I were foundlings. We do not know anything about our past."

Erik remained silent waiting for her to speak.

"If I help ye with information, would ye help me and my brother leave and begin life anew elsewhere?" She swallowed visibly.

He recalled the young man from the first time he'd seen her and wondered why he was not with her.

"Where is yer brother?"

"He is working for Hamish, the old man ye met," she replied, her tone holding a soft lilt that sounded almost like a song.

Erik was no fool. Pretty women were often used to draw men into doing foolish things. The lass was obviously not highly regarded considering the name the injured man called her and was probably seeking information for her people using the ploy of wishing to help.

"We do not require spies. If ye are looking to earn easy coin, unlike the men who were here before, we do not require whores either."

The slap turned his face sideways. Erik was caught off guard for a moment but then grabbed her wrist and yanked her forward. "Do not ever strike me, wench."

"I-I did not mean to do it." She blinked away tears. "I tire of being judged and called names. I am not a whore, sir. I work for my coin honestly…" She stopped talking and yanked her hand free of his grasp. "Forget what I asked. What does it matter? Ye have already formed an opinion of me."

When she took a few steps, Erik called to her, "Wait."

Esme turned and faced him, chin hitched. "I do not require yer help, sir. I will find a way without it."

"Why do ye wish to leave yer village? Tell me." For some reason, Erik did not want her to leave. He wanted to know more about her.

He was aware it was a perilous game. Many a war was won

or lost because of the fairer sex. He had to be careful when dealing with Esme, who had no surname. Either she was telling him the truth or was an accomplished liar.

"I am constantly under threat. My brother, Laith, and I fight every day for food. Laith is very young and does his best." She sighed. "We are capable of looking after ourselves. I do not know why I approached ye, except that I heard yer laird is a fair man."

"He is."

She turned to look over her shoulder toward her village. "Ye should go. They will be returning to the forest from that direction soon. If ye go the way ye came, it should be safe."

With that, she once again hurried away. A short distance from where they'd talked, she gathered up a bundle of branches and continued on her way.

She had been rather close to Clan Ross lands. From where he was, it was a short walk to an area where he could spot the camp where he lived. Erik wondered how often Esme had gone across the shallow portion of the creek and spied.

The offer to work for him meant she was already comfortable with gathering information. Perhaps the only reason she'd spoken to him was that it would have been impossible for her to get away without him catching a glimpse of her. It had been her way of getting out of the situation.

Although Erik was fond of women, he had little reason to trust them. Experience had imparted what treacherous creatures they could be. Once he'd been naïve, he'd given himself body and soul to a woman who'd not only betrayed him but had done so with his own brother.

After finding out Erik cared for the wench, his brother,

Aleksander, had promptly ended things. However, the sting of the discovery had hurt Erik more than any battle injury.

Married and with bairns now, Aleksander lived on the Isle of Skye with their parents. Erik had left and gone to North Uist, needing to get away from the memories. He'd planned to return to Skye one day, but he loved the life of a warrior and decided to remain on Uist.

THE MEN WERE lined up and Auley and his assistant were serving last meal when he returned to the guardhouse.

Erik got in line and while waiting for his turn, his mind kept going back to the woman at the creek.

Esme.

He would return and seek her out. Perhaps asking her to procure information would be a way to get closer to finding out who was in charge of the village and why they allowed or ordered men to keep travelers away.

Something was wrong with a people who remained so secluded. In his opinion, there was usually a bad reason for it.

He joined Torac at a table. "We must speak. I think there may be a way to get information without putting our men at risk."

CHAPTER FOUR

E SME SWUNG WILDLY as she was dragged forward by the hair. She'd barely gotten a glance at the man who had a firm grip on the back of her hair. It was Tavon's brother, Fergus, this time.

"Let me go," she cried out digging her fingernails into his fleshy hand. "Stop at once."

Out of the corner of her eye, she could see people gathering to watch as she was pulled toward the cottage where the council met.

She managed to kick her attacker in the leg, and he stumbled. Unfortunately, he did not release her hair. Snickers from the villagers enjoying the scene made her heart ache. Why did no one help her?

When Fergus half dragged her into the cottage, she fell to the floor landing on her knees and fought to regain her breath.

"There is no need to mistreat the lass," someone said.

Having to swipe the hair from her eyes, she couldn't see who was in the room. After a moment she managed to scramble to her feet and saw that several councilmen had gathered.

"I saw her talking to a Ross warrior," Fergus explained. "She seemed quite friendly with him."

An older man, Rafe, looked her up and down, his upper lip

in a snarl. "What were ye offering him? Selling yerself for coin?"

Esme kept quiet, unsure of what Fergus had seen and if he'd overheard anything. Instead, she looked to the men seated around a table in the dim room. The remnants of a meal remained atop the surface. Most of the food appeared quite unappetizing.

"I was collecting firewood when he happened upon me. All he did was ask my name and how I fared."

At this, Fergus huffed. "She is lying. A man of his stature does not talk pleasantries with a peasant."

The elder of the councilmen met her gaze. "What did ye tell him?"

Esme moved farther from Fergus. "I told him I preferred not to speak to him and then instructed him to leave our lands."

The elder didn't seem to believe her. He looked to the others and one leaned forward and whispered into his ear.

There was a beat of silence, then the council began discussing how to best proceed.

"We can meet with him," someone suggested.

"Ensure they remain off our lands," another recommended.

Fergus gave Esme an amused look. "Or we can send her to gather information. We need to know how many there are and what their plans are."

"I will give ye information in exchange for coin," Esme met one of the men's gazes. "I will require time…"

The sounds of a struggle made everyone turn their attention to the doorway. Two men dragged Laith in. His nose was bloody and one of his eyes was swollen shut, still he continued to try to get away.

Her blood turned to fire, and she ran toward the two who held her brother. Unfortunately, she didn't reach them because Fergus grabbed her from behind.

She held out a hand toward Laith. "Stop fighting. It will be all right."

"I do not trust ye. I have heard things about ye that make me hesitant, so I decided to ensure ye cooperated," Rafe replied. "Laith will remain as my guest until ye get all the information we require."

She whirled toward the councilmen. "Why do ye mistreat my brother and I so? We have never done anything wrong."

Apparently her having spoken to the blond man made them mistrust her. Esme let out a shaky breath. "Ye must promise not to hurt him worse."

Rafe's eyebrows rose at her daring to make a demand. "Of course," he finally replied slowly. His gaze moved to Fergus. "Let her go."

A different councilman, this one older looked her over. "Go now and do as ye are told."

MOMENTS LATER, ESME stumbled into the cottage. Mege sat in the chair slumped over, sleeping. With no one to help her, the elderly woman was unable to stand without losing her balance. At least she'd remained in the chair and had not tried to get up.

The old woman opened her eyes to look at Esme. "What happened? Ye look hurt."

"I tripped and fell in the forest," Esme lied. "Let us get ye cleaned up and I will prepare something to eat."

It was hard to keep from sobbing and screaming and raging over the fact Laith was being held by the council. If only there was a way to escape with Mege. But the woman was much too fragile, much too sickly to travel.

While she cooked eggs, all Esme could think about was what to do. Surely the council had already sent someone to spy on the Ross warriors. There was no need for her to go. If they sent her, it was because they were planning something. The council was using her to perhaps draw the Ross men out so they could be either captured or killed.

As soon as the sun rose, she would go to the camp and try to speak to the blond man again. If only she could trust that they would help her rescue Laith. But why should they?

The next day, she would tell the council the truth. She would tell them the number of warriors and what the blond leader had already told her. Nothing that she'd learned would bring them to consider the Ross warriors as an enemy. Surely they already knew why they had come. After all the attacks on innocent people who traveled near, how could they not Laird Ross not to react?

No matter what else the council had planned, she could only pray once she did as they asked, they would release Laith.

THE OLD WOMAN looked at her with expectation. "Tell me about the forest and the creek. Is it still beautiful?"

"Aye, of course. The creek's clear waters make a soft bubbling noise as it winds through the rocks. Despite it being so late in the season, there are bright green grasses growing in between the trees. In the mornings the sun's rays make it look as if fairies have spent the night decorating."

Mege smiled. "I loved to run through the forest when I was younger."

"Would ye like to go on an adventure? We can go to the seashore," Esme urged. "We can put ye on the back of a wagon."

The woman's hazy gaze took her in. "The sea. Oh, how I loved it. Nay, I can no longer leave the cottage. My bones ache too much and I find it hard to breathe." Her face brightened. "But ye should go and return to tell me all about it."

Esme sighed. Somehow, she had to come up with a plan to leave. There was no choice, they would have to escape. Otherwise, things could become more and more dangerous. Being that she and her brother had no family to defend them, they were easy prey for the council.

THE SUN PEEKED through the trees sending rays through the mist to the wet grass below and Esme recalled her description to Mege. The scene was serene and lovely. Her feet sunk into the ground that was still damp from the rains the night before.

The chilled wind seeped through her worn shawl as Esme made her way to the familiar hidden path that led to where she could see the Ross camp. Hopefully no one else had found the path and it would be easy to traverse unseen.

Birds called out announcing they'd risen for the day. Replies came from other treetops and before long, the forest was filled with song. If not for the grim reason behind her early morning walk, Esme would have appreciated the beauty that surrounded her.

Upon coming to the edge of the woods, she lowered and peered through the branches of a short—but thick—bush.

Men ambled around the campfire, most seeming to have just awakened and were seeking its warmth. A few on horseback looked to be returning from patrolling, by the way they quickly dismounted and guided their steeds to the shelter.

The blond man was nowhere in sight, and she wondered who else was in charge. From her location it was hard to hear anything that was said.

Scanning the area, Esme tried to figure out how to get closer without being seen and perhaps hear what was being discussed.

The breaking of branches made her breath catch and she quickly took inventory of the surroundings. Whoever or whatever approached did not seem to care if they were overheard. If it turned out to be a wild boar, she would have to run to the camp to ensure not being killed.

A few moments later, again the sounds of rustling caught her attention. Esme held her breath as the trickle of fear trailed down her back.

RIGHT THEN A man on horseback appeared at the camp, it was him, the blond warrior. He dismounted and led his horse to the shelter. Esme noted that behind the shelter there was a smaller building from which smoke emanated. Probably the kitchen.

If she could reach the kitchen, then she could possibly get to the horse shelter without being seen.

Though at the moment she could not move, whatever was

in the forest nearby would be alerted to her presence. Crouching down, she crawled deeper into the bush and waited silently. When there was no sound for a few moments, she scrambled from the bush and made her way slowly along the wood's edge hoping to get as close as possible to the kitchen.

Right behind her, the snorts of a hog turned her blood to ice, but she continued going. A split second later, the hog rushed forward.

Esme had to press her lips together to keep from screaming.

Just then a second hog appeared. Apparently the first animal was encroaching, and the hogs began to battle.

All the noise caught the attention of the Ross warriors, who grabbed their swords and their bows, and arrows and rushed to where the hogs fought.

Esme darted from the woods and hurried toward the kitchen. When she spied the blond man brushing down his horse behind the building, she let out a breath of relief.

"I must speak to ye," she whispered. "I require help."

He turned and met her gaze making her chest squeeze at the reminder that he saw her as no more than a lowly peasant. A whore even.

Walking closer so that no one would hear, he bent to speak to her. "What is it? How did ye manage to get past the men?"

"I came to speak to ye. I-I was chased by a boar and the men heard the hogs fighting…" Esme knew she sounded like a mad woman. In her haste to help Laith, she'd not come up with a reason to speak to the blond man. "I wished to offer help once again. The council knows about ye and yer men."

He shrugged. "Of course they do, we are not hiding."

"They wish me to tell them how many of ye there are and what yer plans are."

For a moment he looked past her, as if in thought, then met her gaze. "Tell them we will meet with them. They must come to our land, there at the edge of the forest, ye seem to know so well."

"When?" Esme wondered if what she'd relate would be enough for the council to be satisfied. "Should I give them the exact number of men?"

His glacial gaze met hers again and Esme sucked in a lungful of air. Something about the man affected her. It was as if she'd known him before.

"It matters not. As I said, we are not hiding." His brows gathered. "Why do they send ye and not anyone else? Does no one fear for yer safety?"

A tightening in her chest made Esme flinch. "My brother and I have no one who cares about our wellbeing. I am not a big loss to anyone other than him and Mege."

When his gaze lowered, it was as if he considered what to say next. Upon lifting and looking at her, he studied Esme with interest. "If ye were part of my clan, I would very much ensure no harm came to ye."

He patted her shoulder awkwardly and then turned and stalked away, leaving her to figure out how to get back without being caught.

After looking around and finding no one in sight, Esme turned and hurried back the way she'd come. She'd barely gotten past the kitchen when two warriors came upon her. They took her by the arms.

"Torac, look what we found," one said seeming to find

humor in the situation. "Should we toss her into the creek?"

A muscled warrior walked closer and met her gaze for a moment before turning toward the larger building. "Take her to the forest and release her. She is not a threat."

He then met her gaze. "Stay away. There is nothing to gain here. If I see ye again, I will pierce ye through myself."

Esme began crying. It was all too much, not only being threatened by these unknown people, but also by her own. What had she done to deserve so much mistreatment?

"What are ye doing?" The blond man stalked toward them. "Why is she crying? Did ye harm her?" He glared at the men who held her by the arms. One released her immediately.

The man, Torac, grunted. "I told her to stay away. Never touched a hair on her head. She began crying for no reason."

"Ye did threaten to pierce her through," the man who still held her by the arm said in a jovial tone.

Esme turned her head to wipe her nose on the sleeve of her dress, her shawl had half fallen off. "Let me go," she said between sobs. "I will not return."

"I will take her," the blond man said pulling her from the others. "Stop crying," he snapped. "No one is going to hurt ye."

With his hand on her elbow, he walked toward the forest, his long strides had her nearly running in order to keep up.

When she shivered and attempted to pull her shawl up over her shoulder, he stopped and waited.

"It is best ye do not return. I cannot be everywhere to defend ye if one of my men decides to hurt ye. Do ye understand?" His voice was softer, gentler.

Esme nodded and wiped the tears from her face. "Aye."

"Good."

He surprised her by pulling the cloak from his shoulders and placing it over hers. "Now go on. Go home."

The thick fabric was warm and smelled of him. Esme had never owned anything as well-made. It amazed her how it instantly warmed her fully and she held it tightly around herself.

"What is yer name?" she asked just as she was about to dart into the trees.

He looked at her for a moment. "Erik."

ONCE ESME NEARED her village, she managed to keep from crying. She stopped at her cottage just long enough to check on Mege and leave the warm cloak. Anyone seeing her with it would assume she'd given herself to the man in exchange for it.

Upon arriving at Rafe's cottage, he waved her in and sent a lad to fetch the others.

It seemed to take forever before they finally appeared. Tavon walked in seeming to have recovered from his injuries, although he limped noticeably. He looked her over but didn't seem as interested in her as usual.

Probably still in pain. The thought made her glad.

"What information do ye bring?" Rafe finally asked with a bored expression.

"I saw ten and four men. Warriors, archers, and two cooks." Esme swallowed and looked to the door hoping that Laith would be brought.

"What else?" someone asked.

"Where is my brother?" Esme replied meeting the elder's

gaze. "I wish to see him."

Tavon grunted. "Headed home is my guess."

Relief filled her. "They wish to meet with ye. Ask that ye come to their land, to the camp."

"Is that it?" The elder studied her. "What else?"

"Ye must know the reason they came was because of the unprovoked attacks on travelers. Laird Ross ordered they come and restore safety for their people. That is all I know."

When no one spoke, Esme waited to be told to leave. Finally, Rafe said, "Tell them we will meet them in three days, and we will come to them."

"I was told not to return, or they'd kill me." Esme was prepared to beg. She had no doubt the warrior who'd threatened her would follow through. "Send someone else."

Tavon laughed. "Why should we? They know ye."

"They threatened…" Esme began.

"I am sure they will not. After all, I am sure they expect a response," Rafe said in a flat tone. "Away with ye."

CHAPTER FIVE

I T WAS LATE in the day when Erik and his men reached the
shoreline. In the distance, fishing boats bobbed in the calm
waters, and the smoke from the tiny cottages formed thin lines
against the background of the hills.

The village, Taernsby, was not far. A few hours ride. He
had spent many months there working to restore the damage
after a storm and then remained when a ship had wrecked
offshore.

Erik looked toward the open sea, inhaling the salty air that
always gave him a sense of peace. As he'd grown up on the
shores on the western edge of Skye, thoughts of the cool winds
whipping his hair about as he raced up and down the seashore
collecting shells and rocks came back to him.

It was always a fun day when his father would make a fire
and they'd cook the fish he and Aleksander had caught. As a
wee lad Erik rarely fished, having too much energy for any
activity that required patience.

"This would be a way to get closer to Creag without being
seen," Balgair said bringing his horse alongside. "However,
there is little cover from attack."

Erik looked toward the trees. "Arrows can reach us here
but would not be as accurate."

Just then a group of horsemen appeared. Erik counted

four. He had five with him. Upon them nearing, he drew his weapon until he got a closer look. They were Clan Ross. He and his men sheathed their swords.

"We require yer help," one said. "I am Gavin McKiernan. While on patrol, my men were attacked."

He and his five joined Gavin and his men, and together they rode into the forest, where Clan Ross warriors battled.

"Who are they?" Erik asked Gavin while drawing out his sword.

"I do not know," the warrior replied before charging forward and joining the fray.

Balgair let out a primal yell and urged his steed into a gallop. Some of the enemies were on horses, others on foot. Erik wasn't sure who was who as he only recognized a few men from Clan Ross.

He dismounted and went after one of the two who fought a familiar man.

The sounds of metal against metal rang through the air accompanied by the grunts and screams of fighters.

Clan Ross was outnumbered, but not by many. Although the attackers were more in number, they were not as accomplished fighters.

Erik faced off against a burly man who snarled. "Who are ye?" Erik asked bringing down his sword and then blocking a swipe in return. "Why are ye on our lands?"

"These are not yer lands," the man retorted swinging his sword and barely missing Erik's neck. Somehow Erik managed to cut across the man's shoulder before whirling around to fend off another fighter.

Seeming stunned for a moment, the burly man's eyes

bulged. Then he charged forward blindly, Erik rolled to the ground just as the two enemies clashed, impaling one another.

The burly man howled in anger, pulling his sword from the other man who dropped to the ground.

"I will kill ye!" he yelled and rushed at Erik, catching him around the waist and tackling him to the ground.

All air was knocked out of him and Erik fought to breathe. It was impossible with the heavy man atop him.

The man lifted up and held his sword above his head. It would be a fatal strike, Erik realized as all he could do was move his head and nothing else.

Just then a look of shock overtook the burly man's face and he fell sideways.

Balgair peered down on Erik. "Ye can thank me later." With that, the warrior let out another yell and rushed back into the fray.

When the men who fought the Clan Ross warriors turned and ran, they did not give chase. It would be of little use as most of the Ross men were injured or too exhausted to do so.

Erik sat up and dragged himself to a nearby tree. From the pain when he took a breath, one or two of his ribs were injured. The burly man had landed on him so hard; it had almost struck him unconscious.

"They are Scottish, but not from our isle," Balgair said walking up. "Why are they on our lands?"

Gavin joined them, a huge knot forming on the side of his forehead. "Upon first approaching, they claimed to be settling in the area, for Clan Robertson."

"The Robertson?" Erik gasped out the words. "It cannot be true. The clan is not from the isles."

The last thing they needed was to fight two battles at the same time. If these men were trying to claim a section of the isle for themselves, the laird would have to be informed immediately.

"Has word been sent to the laird?" Erik asked.

"Nay, not as yet. We just now happened upon them," the warrior replied. "I must see about my men." He hurried away as Balgair kneeled next to Erik.

"Gave ye quite a wallop." Despite his bloodthirsty inclination, the warrior looked worried. "We should be able to return without running into them."

Erik glanced to where the warriors walked about seeing to the injured. "How are our men?"

Barely sparing a glance over his shoulder Balgair shrugged. "None of their injuries will be fatal."

How the man had observed it all while fighting was incredible. Of all the men he was glad to have on his side, it was Balgair. They'd fought alongside each other many times. The man was ruthless in battle and rarely lost.

"Help me up," Erik held out his hand and Balgair pulled him to his feet. The pain was not as bad when he was upright, and he prayed it meant his ribs were only bruised.

They went to meet with the rest of the Ross warriors, deciding it would be best to stick together. Though like Erik and his men, the warriors would be expected back at their posts in Taernsby by sundown.

"Altogether, I have twenty and four men," Erik said meeting Gavin's gaze trying to recall if they'd ever fought together.

"How many men are left at Taernsby?"

Gavin shook his head. "There are less now. We will have

ten and five who can fight."

"Ye should ask for more warriors," Balgair stated. "We do not know if that was all of them. There were at least thirty. Given we only killed five, there is nothing to say they did not go to fetch more."

"Aye," Erik said. "Return to Taernsby. My men and I will go back the way we came to our post near Welland. Both of us should remain near our areas until we hear from the laird."

"Agreed," Gavin said and turned to see that a pair of injured warriors were being helped to mount. "As soon as I return to my post, I will send word to the laird."

"Nay, I have more men," Erik stated. "I will send the messenger."

Gavin nodded. "Thank ye."

ERIK AND HIS men rode back to their guardhouse as fast as they could, keeping to Ross lands, but hidden in case the Robertsons returned. The trip back to the camp seemed to take forever as Erik could barely wait for them to arrive so he could stop jostling about.

By the time the camp came into view, he was sweating profusely, and his breathing shallow to keep the pain at bay.

Thankfully, Balgair called warriors to help him and the other injured dismount. The gruff man neared. "Ye are bleeding."

"I am?"

"Aye, someone cut yer back."

Before Erik could reply everything went black.

WHEN ERIK WOKE, it was bright outside. He squinted toward

the window. Not exactly sure how badly he was injured, he did not move.

"Ye are awake." A woman walked in. He recognized her as Helene, the Welland constable's wife. "They brought ye here two days ago. Ye were very ill."

"Two days?" He reached for a cup she held, noting that his hand shook. "What happened to me?"

Helen held the cup to his lips to help him take a drink. "Ye passed out and did not come 'round. Yer men thought ye would die, so they brought ye here to the village."

"I need to return to camp." Erik tried to sit up, but his body felt as if laden with stones. "Why can I not move?"

The woman peered down at him. "Ye require more rest."

"Can ye send for one of my men? Either Balgair or Torac. I must speak to them."

The woman gave him a stern look. "They come to see ye usually in the evening. No need to send for 'im. The man, Torac, comes daily."

Erik grunted and managed to move enough to halfway sit up. Helene stuffed a pillow behind his shoulders. "There is a wound on yer lower back. 'Tis healing but will require some seeing to."

"I appreciate what ye have done. Thank ye."

Seeming satisfied, Helen nodded. "I will bring ye something to eat. Try to rest. There is nowt ye can do right now that will prove more useful."

BY THE TIME Torac arrived, Erik felt much better. It was amazing how rest was often what a person needed after an injury. The wound on his back pulled when he stood and dressed, but other than that, even his ribs did not hurt as much.

He was purple and blue across the chest and arms, there were a pair of bruises on the side of his face and his lip was split. All of it normal after a battle. He winced when he drank the hot concoction Helene had made, as his cut lip protested.

"Ye look like someone dragged ye behind a horse," Torac said all the while studying him. "A message arrived from the laird. He sent twenty men to Taernsby. We cannot assist. He wishes us to remain on course with Creag."

Erik nodded. "I expected more men to be sent."

"They are still patrolling the northern shores and searching for any rebels who may remain. It is a slow process."

"Aye, I understand. But this is a bloody insurgence. What if they bring more?" Erik could not contain his ire. "And here we are ordered to remain and see about a few lurkers in trees."

Without a word, they walked out to a tidy front room. Helene sent Erik a worried look, but seeming to know he would not remain, did not urge him to return to bed.

"Thank ye," he told the woman giving her a pair of coins. "I feel much better."

"Try to rest," the woman said and handed him a small sack. "Ask yer cook to boil these, it will help with the pain. Made into a poultice it will also help with the bruising and healing."

Outside the day was still sunny, the temperate breeze promising warmer weather ahead. Erik took a deep breath only to cringe when his ribs protested. Torac had brought his steed and he mounted.

"How did ye know I would be prepared to leave?" Erik

asked.

"Have brought him every day, just in case."

They rode toward the camp, going the long way so they could patrol the western lands and ensure nothing untoward occurred. As they turned inland toward the forest, Erik thought of something.

"The lass. Ye know the one who I escorted away?"

Torac nodded.

"Has she returned?"

"Not that I have seen. Ye warned her off did ye not?"

"I did not expect her to listen. She seemed desperate."

They guided the horses into the tree line. Torac scanned the area, then looked to him. "Ye know it is probably a ploy to get ye to let yer guard down."

"I do." Erik paused before adding, "Let us go closer to the village and have a look."

Torac shrugged and they continued forth.

Moments later, through the trees, just past the creek, he could see the cottage where the old man, Hamish, lived. There didn't seem to be anyone about.

Then as if conjured just a moment later, the lass appeared. She carried a basket of clothes that she threw over a line to dry.

Erik let out a long whistle and she stilled and looked toward the trees. She could probably make out their horses. If she did, Esme did not react.

"She does not expect us," Torac said with a grunt. "Caught her off guard."

They waited as she first looked over her shoulder toward the small cottage and then raced to the front door, picked up a smaller basket, and ambled toward them.

"I will remain on this side of the creek," Torac said. "Be with care."

Dismounting, Erik handed the reins to Torac and walked to the creek's edge. Then he hopped on rocks until reaching the other side. Once there, he remained beside a tree until Esme approached.

"Ye should be with care," she hissed. "They expect that I will speak to ye and have been watching me."

She bent and plucked some plants and placed them in her basket. Then she walked a few feet away and repeated the action. "They wish to come to yer camp but want assurances of safe passage."

"When?"

"Tomorrow."

She moved closer, then past him, once again bending and collecting more plants to give the illusion of not speaking to anyone.

"All I am doing is telling ye what they wish. I want to leave, my brother and me. We cannot until Mege, who we care for, is strong enough to do so."

It was not his concern what the lass wished to do. All he cared about at the moment was whether or not he could acquire peace in the area so he and his men could help with the other issue.

When she walked closer, he took her arm. Seeming startled by his touch, Esme stumbled and fell forward against him. The parting of her plump lips was a siren call to his basic instinct. It was annoying that she awakened a part of him that had been dormant for far too long.

He wanted the lass and was man enough to admit it. However perfect the opportunity was, he could not do anything about it. Not with Torac looking on.

"I just wish to live in peace. It can never be, not here in this village," she said in a low voice, not moving away from him.

He could help her. But not at the moment. It would be an open invitation for the council to keep from negotiating peace with Clan Ross.

"I cannot help ye lass."

She lowered her face. "Then I will do it without anyone's help."

Needing to reassure her, he lifted her face and upon seeing that she cried could contain himself no longer. Erik covered her mouth with his, fire igniting through his body like never before. It was as if she was the one he'd been waiting for. A missing piece of him that was returned after being lost for a lifetime. She tasted of home, of familiarity, and yet also of something new.

Esme backed away and brought her hand to her mouth, her gaze locked with his.

"Why did ye do that?" There was something akin to hurt in her gaze. He recalled the name the injured man had called her.

"Because ye are beautiful. I apologize for taking such liberty. Please forgive me." Eric bent, plucked a wildflower, and held it out to her. "I should not have kissed ye."

With barely a nod of acceptance, she took the flower and dropped it into her basket. She looked past him to where Torac stood. "I will tell the council ye assure them safety."

"Esme?" Erik said. "Be with care."

"I will, Erik," she whispered as she backed away. Then hurried away in the direction of her cottage.

It took a moment for Erik to compose himself. The way she'd said his name, as if she too recognized what had occurred between them in that moment. The reunion of two souls that belonged together.

"Idiot," Erik mumbled. He was turning a spontaneous simple kiss into a romanticized version of something that wee lasses made up stories about. Thankfully no one would ever know of his thoughts.

Prepared to face whatever Torac would say as the man had effectively witnessed the entire thing, he trudged back across the creek to his steed.

"What did she have to say?" Torac asked as Erik mounted his horse.

"The council plans to come tomorrow. They wish for safe passage."

Torac snorted as they turned and headed back to camp. "We should kill them all. The bastards have killed plenty of our people."

"It would be satisfying. I wonder how many will be left behind to carry on."

Keeping an eye on the surroundings, Torac replied, "It would be a fair warning for them not to continue. Then we can see about the true danger to the isle."

They rode for a bit longer, the camp coming into view. "Our men have completed the smaller guardhouse," Erik said noting that now the small building was finished the men practiced swordplay or ambled about.

"Is that what the kiss was about?" Torac finally asked the question Erik was not quite prepared to answer.

Instead of a reply, he snorted and urged his mount into a

canter. In truth, he wasn't sure why he'd done it. It was a stupid thing to have kissed the lass, now it was all he could think about. How much he wanted to see her again and kiss her again.

Usually he kept away from the fairer sex until his body demanded physical relief, nothing more. And when he had sex, it was with someone he did not find attractive or appealing.

Esme was different. Since the first time he saw her standing up to him, he knew there was something about her that had called to him. A certainty that there had to be something between them.

It was ridiculous of course. And the main reason why warriors on duty were not permitted to seek relationships. He would punish his men if they were caught courting when on orders from the laird.

Erik considered how he would punish someone who broke the rules as he'd just done. He waited for Torac to dismount and bring his horse to the shelter. As they brushed down the animals and filled the feed buckets with fresh oats and water for them, he turned to Torac.

"I should not have done it. It was utter stupidity on my part."

Torac's dark gaze met his. "I have never seen ye with a lass. Ye have always been a warrior who works harder than most. 'Tis a bit satisfying to see that even ye can stumble." The man had the audacity to chuckle. "The wee lass has managed to pierce yer armor."

"She has not," Erik stated blowing out a breath. "It was nothing."

"Good, otherwise it could be a problem."

At the sound of horses approaching, they walked out to greet the men who returned from patrol. Lads who'd been hired from the village rushed to take the steeds as the men looked tired and about to fall from them.

The warriors had left at dawn, meaning they'd been riding for an entire day. The horses were more animated than the men. Probably from the prospect of food and shelter.

"After we meet with the council, I am giving our men a day off to rest and go to the village." Torac walked toward the warriors to listen to their report.

Erik went to the men who were about to leave. They were ten in total, five who were to patrol to Welland and the other five to the smaller village and the farms.

"Do not go near the southern shore," Erik instructed the men.

Torac spoke to Balgair, as the man mounted in preparation to leave. "Stay away from Creag."

Although a man of few words, Balgair was a good leader and strong warrior. The man's hazel gaze met Erik's. "There is no reason for us to, as we head north. Why are we patrolling the areas that are on Ross lands? It seems a waste of time."

"I agree," Erik said in a low voice so only Balgair could hear. "But 'tis what the laird ordered."

The warrior nodded and looked to his men. "Mount!"

CHAPTER SIX

H E'D KISSED HER. It had been like a dream, something she'd not ever imagined happening to her. To be kissed by such a handsome man. A stranger if she were honest, but still it was a sweet kiss. Erik had not expected anything in return. He wanted to show to her that he found her attractive. Esme wasn't sure how she knew, but she did.

If only it had lasted longer. This one and only happenstance.

Esme's heart threatened to burst from her chest when she neared the village square. Still carrying the basket with what turned out to be mostly weeds, she didn't bother stopping to look for Lattie. The sooner she got it over with, the better.

Once she gave the council the message that they had safe passage to the Ross camp, she would begin to plan her escape.

"Come lass," a man called from the doorway of the tavern. "I have some work for ye."

Despite being in a hurry, Esme could not turn down the opportunity to earn some money. "What can I do for ye, Colin?" she said nearing, but not daring to get too close to the man else the villagers begin more rumors about her.

"My wife is ill. I need someone to sweep the floors and clean the tabletops." He gave her a cursory once over. At the lack of interest, Esme felt more comfortable walking closer.

She nodded enthusiastically. "I can do it, but first I must see the council. I will return at once and begin to work."

The man gave a curt nod and looked toward Rafe's cottage. "Be with care." When noting that the man actually worried for her, it was hard not to cry. Usually no one seemed to be bothered with her, one way or another.

"I will return shortly," Esme called out and continued to councilman Rafe's house. Once again her breathing hitched with fear.

After a couple of knocks a woman opened the door. Esme knew her to be Rafe's wife, a cruel woman who often called her names.

"What do ye want?" The woman's eyes narrowed.

"I-I must speak to yer husband."

When the woman's gaze swept over her and a sneer formed, Esme wanted to turn and leave.

"See that is all ye do. Talk." The woman opened the door barely leaving enough space for Esme to squeeze through.

"Who is it?" Rafe called out, then he sat up straighter in his chair when noting who it was.

"I came to tell ye, safe passage to the Ross camp is assured."

The man looked to his wife before replying. "What else?"

"Nothing. I could not get close enough to the camp to see or hear anything. They threatened to kill me if I went there. I managed to get the attention of the blond man, their leader, I believe, as he took his horse to the creek to drink."

Rafe huffed. "I believe only half of what ye say. Why would they threaten to kill ye? Ye are insignificant. However, ye do seem to have a quick wit about ye."

Hoping he had nothing else planned for her, Esme fidgeted.

Rafe looked to his wife. "Ye could do with being smarter like the lass."

Esme flinched as if he'd said it to her. It was she who'd pay for the cruel remark. The woman would ensure it.

When he didn't speak to her again, she turned wanting to leave quickly before he asked more of her.

"If I require ye again, I will send word," he called out as she walked out the door past the glaring woman who slammed it behind her.

Once in the tavern, Esme hurried about the tasks that had to be done. She worried about leaving Mege for so long. Hopefully, Hamish's wife would stop by as she often did when out for a walk.

It was already late in the day and Mege had only eaten that morning.

The aroma of the stew cooking and baked bread made her stomach growl loudly, and she did her best to keep from looking directly at the bowls people ate out of.

She cleaned tables, washed dishes, and served food. Whenever there was a spare moment, she swept the floor and even fed scraps to a pair of dogs that hovered near the back door.

Hours later, after clearing dirty dishes from table after table and washing them all, she went to a corner to wait for a pair of men to leave so she could clean the last one.

Colin motioned her over. "Make yerself a bowl. It will be a bit yet before they leave. Ye may as well eat."

It was hard not to rush to ladle stew into the bowl as her mouth watered in anticipation. Moments later with the food in front of her, Esme almost swooned with delight. She could not recall a better meal in a long, long time. Crusty bread smothered in freshly churned butter and hot lamb stew with fat carrots and potatoes in a rich thick sauce flavored with onions and herbs.

Esme ate every bit of it, sopping up any remaining sauce with a piece of bread. If not for others being present, she would have probably licked the bowl. Once she finished eating, guilt set in at the thought that neither Laith nor Mege could share such a wonderful meal.

"Clean up the cooking area," Colin said as he walked by carrying two tankards of ale to the men who showed no signs of leaving.

It was late in the evening when she was finally able to leave.

The tavern owner paid her well, and at seeing the coins he gave her, she was once again overcome with gratitude. "Should I return on the morrow?"

After considering for a moment, the man nodded. "Aye, my Claire is quite unwell."

He looked over his shoulder at a pair entering. "Go on now lass. Come around midday, I can handle the morning alone with my lad."

Outside the sun had sunk low into the horizon leaving just enough light for her to see. The village square was empty, as people had gone home to prepare for the night. She hurried past several cottages, giving Tavon's home a wide berth.

Finally, at the sight of her cottage, she almost cried with relief at seeing a light through the open doorway.

Upon entering, she found Laith and Mege at the table

eating what looked to be soup.

"Who cooked?" Esme asked peering into the bowls finding it to be fish stew.

"Hamish's wife," Laith replied. "I saved some for ye."

Esme kissed his cheek. "I worked at the tavern and had the most delicious meal. I feel badly not to have dared asked for some to bring home."

Her brother shook his head, not seeming to care in the least. "I am glad ye had a good meal sister. This fish stew is quite delicious and knowing ye are not hungry means there's a second bowl for me."

While Esme fed Mege, she told Laith about working in the tavern and about giving a message to Rafe. "I hope to be able to work at the tavern a few more days. It will go far in saving for when we leave."

The entire time she talked, Laith kept his gaze downcast. It was obvious he did not wish to get his hopes up.

They had to wait until Mege died, which meant, they had no way of knowing how long it would be before the possibility of leaving would happen.

Esme studied the old woman who gave her a toothless soft smile. "How do ye feel today Mege? Were ye alone long?"

The woman shook her head. "Nay. I had company. Tavon came by and then—"

Esme's breath caught. "What did he want?"

"Asked where ye went and said he had plans and soon we would be living with 'im."

Exchanging looks with her brother, the silent message they would discuss it after putting Mege to bed.

"What else did Tavon say?" Esme asked the old woman

who shook her head not wishing to eat more.

After considering, Mege frowned. "Said he didna care that ye sell yerself for coin." Mege huffed. "I told 'im ye are a good lass. He didna believe me."

"He's an idiot," Esme said. "Did he frighten ye?"

Mege shook her head. "I am not scared of 'im or his father. All of them are daft."

Both Laith and Esme laughed at Mege's words. The mirth was short-lived when Mege began coughing until blood stained her lips. Once Esme finally got her settled in bed, the tired old woman instantly fell asleep.

"Poor thing. I hope she rests well," Esme said. "Laith can ye remain home tomorrow? I made more coin at the tavern than ye make working with Hamish's son."

Laith shook his head and peered to where Mege slept. "I cannot. We are almost finished with the pig's pen. I can ask the missus to come and see about her."

"Fine. I will leave midday and not return until late."

KNOWING THE MEN from the village of Creag were to come to meet with them, Torac and Erik kept the men at the camp.

Seeming to want to give the impression Clan Ross was not a priority, it was late morning before the councilmen from Creag finally appeared.

To give the illusion of having more men, only Erik, Torac, and five men mounted. They left horses visible in a corral, while a group of men sparred. Another group of guards rode in the near distance where it would make it hard to know how many there were.

Auley and his lad had donned warrior clothes and brushed down horses on the side of the shelter where they were visible.

It seemed to work because the councilmen kept their distance, stopping on the edge of the camp. On horseback were three older men, and another four who had swords strapped to their backs. None, except one bearded man, looked like warriors in Erik's estimation.

A short distance away, he noted a few archers remaining near the edge of the forest.

"I am Erik. I represent Laird Darach Ross."

The men before him exchanged looks before one spoke. "We are the village council. Our village of Creag is off limits to yer clan. We are independent of yer laird."

As he didn't give a name, Torac did not identify himself. "We are not here to overtake yer village, but to ensure our people are left in peace when traveling through the forest and to the southern shore."

The man spread his arms, his lips curving into an indulgent smile. "As long as travelers stay away from our land, we do nothing to stop them. If on our lands, we can take precautions to keep our people safe."

Erik wanted to slap the grin from his face. "They must cross the creek to get to the shore, the boundary between our lands is unclear. But those that have been attacked, as well as those that have been killed while traveling through the forest past the creek, have been on Ross lands." He motioned in the direction of the shoreline. "None were on yer land."

This time another man with graying temples spoke. His gaze was direct and flat. "I am called Rafe. We cannot control who attacks people in the forest. Why do ye assume they are from our village and not from yers? The village of Welland is not that far."

"We know they are from yer village. Ye do as well," Balgair snarled, his upper lip twisting. "Hanging from trees, spearing defenseless people with arrows. Bunch of cowards."

At the words, the bearded man grunted. "Sounds like yer clan more than ours."

"What clan would that be?" Erik asked genuinely interested.

"We were once Robertson."

Erik fought not to exchange looks with the others. The same name as the ones they'd battled just the day before. When the fighters had fled, they'd not gone in the direction of the village, but east.

"Can we come to an agreement, that ye will keep the path to the south that falls on our lands free of menace? We will do the same for yer people who may wish to travel to Welland."

"Our people have no need to go anywhere," Rafe instantly replied. "No need at all."

Torac met the man's gaze. "Yer people are imprisoned then?"

The older man who'd spoken at first shook his head. "Of course they're not. What Rafe meant is that we have all we need and are completely independent."

"Who is yer laird?" Erik asked. "Is he here on North Uist?"

"We have no affiliation to the Robertson. We are—"

"Let me guess . . . independent," Balgair said in a flat tone.

The bearded man glared at Balgair. "Aye, not like ye who are controlled by one man. We are not like dogs to be led about."

By the way the two glared at one another, it was obvious that if the two parties ever came to battle, Balgair and the bearded man would attack each other.

Torac spoke next in an even tone. "Alliance to a laird is the way of our people. I would say there is honor in loyalty and protecting the clans' people. We are here to provide protection for the people of Welland, Aldness, and the farmers that are near here as well as any travelers."

Erik met the man Rafe's gaze. "We have been warning our people that if anyone is involved in harming travelers, they will be made to pay. I suggest ye do the same."

"Although we highly doubt it is our people. It will be dealt with," Rafe replied and then met Erik's gaze directly. "Ensure ye stay away from our people."

He wondered if the man meant Esme.

They turned their steeds and galloped away. Only the bearded man turned to look over his shoulder to scowl at Balgair.

"Somehow I do not think it was a productive meeting," Torac grumbled. "They know full well it is their people, possibly even some of them who've been accosting our people."

Erik sent a guard to inform the others to regroup. Meanwhile, he held Torac and Balgair back. "We must find out if they are indeed Robertson's. If connected to the others who we battled, there may be a larger problem at hand than we were expecting."

"I think they lied. If anything they are Macdonalds, not Robertsons," Balgair said.

Erik frowned. "True. But why lie?"

They didn't have an answer, so they let the subject go. In the scheme of things, it mattered little if they claimed a clan or not. It was evident, they were not friends to Clan Ross.

After the midday meal, the guards were given a day of rest. The next patrols would not begin anew until the day after next.

Thinking the best place to find out information would be in the village, Erik and Balgair rode to Welland. With his battle ax across the wide expanse of his back and his shield tied to his horse's saddle, the man kept a stern expression. Although he had fought alongside the man many times, Erik had not gotten to know Balgair well but had heard good things about him.

"Have ye competed against the Ross brothers at the games?" Erik asked, interested to know how Balgair fared against Duncan Ross who often won any strength competition he entered.

Balgair nodded. "Aye, I've beaten Darach once at hammer throw. But never at caber toss, never."

With shortly cropped brown hair and a bearded face, Balgair could have been mistaken for a Ross.

"Are ye related to them?"

"Distant cousin." The hazel eyes met his. "Why?"

"I can see a bit of family resemblance."

"What do ye compete in when at the games?" Balgair changed the subject.

"Stone put."

Erik noted a pair of horsemen coming toward them. Everyone was a stranger to him in that part of the isle, so he kept his guard up and watched them to ensure they did not reach for a weapon.

Upon nearing, the horsemen slowed. "Are ye guards with Clan Ross?" one of the men asked.

"Aye," Erik replied. "Why?"

"The constable wishes to speak to yer leader. He said he was light of hair, is it ye?"

Erik nodded. "We were on our way to see him."

The welcome by the constable was not at all what they expected. The man was at the tavern with two men and several women.

"Sit!" the man shouted. "Enjoy!"

As soon as they sat down, both he and Balgair were joined by women. Two chose Erik. Both with blouses pulled down their shoulders so low, their breasts threatened to spill out.

Tankards of ale were placed before him and he drank deep, enjoying the momentary time away from camp and talk of battles. It could not last, and he would not drink more than the one.

In his role of leadership, he could not allow his guard down.

"Ah!" He spit out the ale when one of the women managed to slide her hand down the front of his breeches and had her hand wrapped around his cock. She leaned forward and pressed her lips to his ear. "I can make ye spill. Ye need it."

He tried to push her hand away, but she had a firm grip. So he gritted his teeth.

Looking across the table he noted that Balgair had a strange expression and wondered if the same happened to him.

He took the woman by the shoulders and pulled her up to stand. Unfortunately, she did not relinquish her hold on him.

"Ah, lass, release him. 'Tis obvious he is not interested at the moment," the constable said laughing loudly.

The others around the table hooted with laughter when she made a show of pulling her hand out and then motioning that he was quite large.

Erik blew out a breath. "Constable, I require a moment of yer time."

"Relax warrior. Ye earned it. I've had a special meal prepared for ye."

At Balgair's loud grunt, Erik didn't have to guess what happened under the table. No one seemed to take much notice. Looking around he wondered how many had been serviced by the women hoping to earn coin.

Just as he was about to ask another question, huge trays of roasted pig and other foods were brought. The constable beamed with pride. "It is our way of thanking ye and yer men."

"It is only two of us today," Erik said unsure why such a grand meal was served for just them.

"The men were sent to invite more," the constable remarked. "Will they come?"

There was an underlying reason for the sudden change in the constable. Although friendly, Erik had not noticed him being so boisterous before. Then again, it was the first time he'd been around the man in the tavern. It could be he acted differently when with his wife.

"A word," Erik stated standing. "Outside."

The constable gave him a perplexed look before standing and following him outside. As soon as they exited, Balgair joined them.

"I came to speak to ye about something serious. At the

moment the lives of the people are at risk. This is not the time to celebrate."

The man seemed crestfallen. "My apologies. I did not wish to offend. Since ye and yer men have arrived the people have felt free to move about without constantly living in fear. It is a reason to celebrate."

Meeting the man's gaze, Erik explained about the new threat of the insurgents and how he wished for the constable to assemble the village so that they could address what happened.

"I must go to Aldness and do the same," Erik finished. "I cannot say that anyone is safe until we find out who the aggressors are."

"At once, of course," the constable replied.

"In the morning is soon enough," Erik stated and then added. "Thank ye for the offer of such a grand meal. I would stay and eat, but we must go to the other village and the farms before sun fall.

Once on the road to Aldness, Erik looked to Balgair. "The wenches were rather persistent."

"Ye were quicker to realize what happened," Balgair replied.

As much as he wanted to laugh, Erik managed to keep a straight face.

THE SMALL VILLAGE of Aldness was picturesque. With cobblestone paths and flower boxes at almost every window. There were only about a dozen scattered cottages, a chapel, and what looked to be a marketplace. In the center of the village was a well that a pack of hounds bounded past with prizes of meaty bones.

Erik and Balgair dismounted and were immediately greeted by a pair of elderly men who waved them over. "Young men. What brings ye through our wee village?"

"Do ye not remember me?" Erik asked one who he'd met on the way to the camp.

The elderly man studied him and began cackling. "Aye, I should. However, I do not."

His companion met Erik's gaze. "Ye are warriors working for the laird. We've not seen the young laird."

"Is there a constable?" Balgair asked impatiently.

"Lars lives there." One of the men pointed to a cottage that was a bit larger than the two on either side.

They walked to the cottage and upon nearing and hearing a man calling out, went to the back. A man, who Erik supposed was Lars, stood inside a fenced-in area feeding the goats and pigs from a bucket.

He looked over to Erik and Balgair and motioned for them to come closer. "Ye return. Is there news?"

"Ye were not here when I rode through. I expected that ye would come to the camp to speak to me by now." Erik wasn't sure what to make of the man who frowned and scratched his head.

"As ye only said yer men were to ensure peace and seek out safe passage, I expected that word would be sent if there was any news."

Instead of correcting the man, Erik let out a breath. "There are aggressors that attacked us near the shoreline, just outside of the lands that belong to the remote village. Have there been any others traveling past here?"

The man emptied the bucket into a small trough and exited the pen. He was dirty from the knees down, his breeches caked with mud and other hard to identify filth.

"There were a group of men who rode through several days ago. They claimed to be Clan Ross and headed from the southern shore to Taernsby. I thought it odd they traveled past here since the village is on the opposite side of the isle."

After going back and forth, it was obvious to Erik the warriors were Clan Ross and traveled from the northwest when called to the post by the laird.

After rinsing his face and hands, the man turned to Erik. "What can I do to help?"

"Keep yer people here for now. We cannot promise safe travels at the moment. We will continue to patrol, but the area is large."

"We can protect ourselves," Lars said. "My son is sword trained and takes time to train the young men to fight."

Erik hoped it would not come to it that the men of the small village would have to fight against the ruthless men they'd battled. However, he kept his thoughts to himself. "I am glad to hear it. Ross men should all be prepared to defend their home."

"Would ye like for me to send someone to see ye regularly?" Lars asked. "I can come meself."

The man was young, perhaps his age of thirty and two. Erik wondered at him having a son old enough to fight. "Ye must have married young."

"Aye, ten and six. My wife the same. We have three sons, the eldest is ten and seven." The man chuckled. "We were too eager to wait."

Erik liked the man. "No need to come to the camp. My

men will be riding through regularly on patrol. They wear the tartan so ye can identify them. If ye see anything that gives ye pause, speak to them when they come by."

"I will," Lars replied.

When they returned to the village square, onlookers had gathered. The people there were a friendly welcoming lot, who seemed excited at travelers coming through.

"THERE ARE SEVERAL farms," Balgair said an hour later as the planted fields came into view. Cows grazed, without a care in the world. Several horses pranced in a corral, their tails swishing side to side.

"I do not think the Robertson fighters came from the north. I would venture to guess they came from the east, sneaking between Taernsby and the empty land before reaching Duncan Ross' lands."

"Aye, I agree." Balgair scanned the area. "This would be out of their way."

It turned out as expected, although happy to see them, the families of the farming community had nothing suspicious to impart. Upon hearing about travelers being attacked, a family informed Erik they planned to travel to visit family in a sennight.

"Come to the camp, we will provide escort," Erik assured them. Finally, hours later they headed toward camp.

TWO DAYS LATER, they'd spoken to the people of Welland and spread the word in the area for people to travel with care.

There were grumblings of disappointment at the lack of protection and Erik could understand their frustration. After all, they were members of the strongest clan in the region. The should be able to travel about without fear.

He would wait a bit more, but then he'd travel to the keep and insist the laird send an army to overtake the troublesome village. It was not fair to the innocent.

Upon reaching camp, Erik noted men riding to the forest's edge. "Come let us see if something is of note."

They rode a short distance away from the men and into the woods. It was eerily silent, a bad sign when the birds did not chirp.

"Movement there," Balgair whispered and pointed to a group of bushes.

It was late in the day and the shadows made it hard to see. The patrolling had taken them to an area far to the west while remaining on the Ross side of the creek.

"Could be a beast," Erik replied holding up a fist to signal for the others to stop. As one, they each turned an ear toward the area, hoping to hear something.

There was a soft whimper.

Immediately Erik dismounted and pulled his sword.

They crept toward the sound of someone crying, expecting that it could be a trap. Balgair held up his battle ax at the ready and stopped to allow Erik to go closer.

There was no mistaking the smell. Spilled blood. He peered into the opening to find a small girl crying. "I mean ye no harm."

The girl clung to a person who lay on their back. It looked to be a man. He was dead.

"No," the girl said and began to cry harder arms out-stretched toward the motionless man. "Da!"

He lifted the child into his arms, and she screamed out in pain. It was then he realized she was also injured. "Take her. I will check the man."

Balgair motioned to another man, who came and took the sobbing girl. "Take her to town. Ensure the woman, Helene, sees her at once."

As he suspected the man was dead. He was young, perhaps just over twenty. He'd been impaled by three arrows, one directly in the center of his chest. Somehow the man managed to drag the little girl into the bushes and then lay in front of her in an effort to keep her safe before dying.

"Bastards," Erik spat on the ground, his blood boiling. "What threat could they have possibly been to them?"

Without another word, he mounted and rode across the creek and directly to the enemy village. It was not until he galloped into the village square that he realized his men had followed behind. Their enormous war horses sent people running in all directions.

People peered out from every door and window, looking to see what they did next.

A man stood at the doorway to a tavern. "I am called Colin, who do ye seek?"

"Yer councilmen," Erik gritted out the words. "Our people have been attacked again. One of them killed." He stood in the center of the village and yelled out the words. "Whoever is killing innocent people will be made to pay."

Three familiar men rushed to where he stood. One he recognized as the man called Rafe, the other the man with the gray on his temples, and lastly the bearded one who'd taken an instant dislike to Balgair.

"Ye have no right to come here and speak to our people," the man Rafe spoke, his face contorted with rage.

"I can have ye killed on the spot." Rafe took several steps back when Balgair moved forward.

Erik spoke to the irritating man. "We asked that ye warn yer people against killing innocents. Today a young man and his daughter were attacked. A child was speared with an arrow."

Rafe met his gaze. With an expression like that of a sly fox, Erik instantly knew he would lie.

"As we told ye. It is not our people who are attacking. We would never stand for it." He shook his head. "A tragedy what occurred."

It took effort to keep from drawing his sword. "When I find out who is doing it, they will die. I know it is a group of men who are too cowardly to face actual warriors. Instead, they prey on the defenseless," Erik called out. "Is that who lives here? Gutless men?"

The bearded man's expression changed; eyes narrowed at Erik before he turned to look over his shoulder at another man who stood next to the tavern owner. It was the man who'd fallen out of the tree and been taken by his men to a cottage.

The two were probably part of the group that was attacking people.

"This is yer one and only warning," Erik said turning on his heel and going to his steed.

"Do not return," Rafe called out.

Balgair rushed to the man, bending over until their noses

touched. "If we return, ye will not like it."

The man Rafe stumbled backward and fell onto his bottom.

When the bearded men started towards Balgair, Rafe stopped him. "Fergus, help me up."

CHAPTER SEVEN

"ONLY SOLD ONE," Esme sighed, and Lattie gave her an understanding look. "There aren't many people out today. The rain is keeping them away."

"I need to find a way to make enough so that we can get Mege hearty, restorative food. She is getting weaker every day."

"She is very old," Lattie replied. "'Tis a wonder she lives still."

"Aye." Esme's chest tightened. "She took us in and cared for us all on her own. I cannot imagine life without my sweet Mege." Blinking away tears, she followed the progress of Rafe's wife as the woman purchased items at another stand.

"Do ye have something for Mege to eat today?" Lattie asked.

Esme was not sure how to respond. They had eggs, but that was all. The hens had only laid two eggs that morning and the three of them had shared the meager meal.

"I do," Esme replied. "With the coin from the basket, I can purchase a potato and some leeks. Laith has gone fishing and hopefully he caught something."

There was understanding in Lattie's face. "Ye both are survivors, I do not doubt ye will find a way."

Tavon exited the tavern and made a beeline for where she

and Lattie stood. "Here comes the idiot," Lattie murmured under her breath.

Esme agreed, the man seemed to live to make her life miserable.

"Did ye get my message?" His half-closed gaze swept over her. "I spoke to the old hag ye live with."

Esme turned away. "Leave me be."

"Did ye?" Tavon insisted.

"If ye have something to tell me then do it," Esme assumed a flat expression. "What is it?"

At her lack of fear or reaction, Tavon seemed confused. "I told her I would take ye for wife. Despite yer reputation in the village."

"Is this the point where Esme should fall to her knees and thank ye?" Lattie said with an incredulous look. "Why would she want ye? What kind of offer is that?"

"'Tis more than any other man has offered, isn't it?" Tavon asked. "She cannot expect much."

"I do not want ye. I can take care of myself." Esme was shaking with anger. It was turning out to be the most horrible day. First the news of yet someone else being attacked in the woods, then earning so little coin, and now this. The only bright spot had been catching a glimpse of Erik as he'd rode past toward the center of town and then again when they'd left the village.

"Ye should consider it," Tavon said. "Things will only get worse for ye. There is nothing to be done about it. Ye really have no choice."

As if to emphasize Tavon's words, the rain became harder, sending a chill through Esme.

Desperate to get away from him, she looked from one side of the village square to the other. The only thing she could think was to go to the tavern, but it would be easy for Tavon to follow her.

Finally, he gave her a pointed look. "Here." He held out a leather bag with a long strap that she could wear across her body. "For when ye collect whatever it is ye do in the forest."

Desperate to get rid of him, Esme grabbed the strap and he walked away; shoulders hunched from the rain.

"Ye should hurry home and remain there. He will not give up easily."

"What is that?"

Esme turned to find Rafe's wife, Tavon's mother, staring at the pouch. "Where did ye get that bag?"

Not in the mood to deal with the woman, Esme turned to Lattie. "I will see ye in a couple of days." She picked up her remaining baskets and rounded the woman who continued staring at the bag.

SHE WAS ALMOST back to her cottage when the realization of where Tavon could have gotten the pouch struck. Did he take it from a dead man? The coincidence was much too large.

The horrible truth caused her breath to catch and the forest before her to blur. Esme stumbled, unable to see clearly where she went.

The entire village was aware of Erik's accusations to the village council. A man and his young lassie had been attacked. Both struck with arrows. The man was dead, and his little girl was injured. Could it be true? Were Tavon and his ilk capable of such cruelty?

The man could not have been carrying anything of value.

Unable to keep walking, Esme sunk to the ground and after throwing the baskets away from her, she yanked the pouch from her shoulder and desperately dug into it unsure of what she sought.

Her fingers curled around something and with a trembling hand, she pulled out a thin white ribbon.

"Oh, no." Shivers traveled up her body, and down her arms until she could not stop from shaking. How was it possible for someone to do such horrible things and then think to gift what they stole? It was as if the man's death meant nothing.

All for what.

Without thinking, Esme jumped to her feet and ran back toward the center of the village. With the pouch hanging from her hand, and the ribbon in her other fist, she searched for Tavon. When he wasn't outside, she went to the tavern next.

He sat with his brother, both looking startled when she approached. The expression on her face must have been murderous by the cautious way both men leaned away.

"Where did ye get this?" Esme asked, her voice tight. "Who did ye take it from?"

Recovering from his initial surprise, Tavon regained his usual careless expression. "What is it to ye? I gave ye a gift, be thankful."

"Ye did it didn't ye? Ye killed that poor man and injured the wee lass. And all ye got was this."

At the accusation the tavern went silent, everyone turning to look at them.

"Ye are a murderer and a thief." Esme threw the pouch

atop the table. It landed halfway into the bowl of whatever Tavon ate. "And for what? A pouch and a ribbon?"

"Be with care about what ye say," Tavon's brother Fergus growled.

Too furious to be afraid, Esme whirled to face the towering man. "Aye, that is what everyone does. Too afraid of the both of ye to do anything."

She turned to Tavon. "She is but a wee thing and has now lost her da because of ye."

Not caring, she rounded Fergus and stalked out of the tavern. Blinded by tears of grief over someone she'd never met, Esme stumbled toward home.

It didn't take long for Tavon and his brother to recover and bent on proving they'd not be bested by a woman. When they caught up with her, Esme held her breath waiting for the beating or worse.

The brothers surrounded her, the looks on their faces deceivingly passive. To an onlooker, it would seem as if they asked about her day.

"Ye will not get away with what ye did," Tavon hissed.

"Aye, ye will pay," Fergus added.

"So ye will kill me then? Or hurt my brother. That is what ye do isn't it?" Esme's voice trembled as she spoke. "Ye like to hurt people."

"I know ye are afraid of me." Tavon grabbed her arm and yanked her forward until there was but a hair's breadth between them. "Ye should be."

"WHAT HAPPENS?" RAFE asked as he slowed his horse. His gaze moved from her to his sons. "Let the lass be. We must speak at once. Come to my house."

When Rafe rode away, Tavon motioned to his brother who grabbed Esme by the arms. Her eyes went wide, unsure what they would do before following their father to his house. Surely they'd not take her in broad daylight.

Tavon leaned over her. "When ye are my wife, I will keep ye in line. Yer mouth will have better things to do than spew accusations."

"Let me go." Esme struggled without luck against the painful hold on her upper arms.

Suddenly, all her breath was gone because Tavon's fist sunk into her stomach, and she let out a loud *oomph* as all the air in her body was viciously pulled from her.

When Fergus released her, she crumpled to the ground unable to do more than roll into a ball, unable to do more than gasp for air.

"See that ye keep yer mouth shut from now on." The brothers ambled away laughing.

"Come on get up." Colin had rushed over to help her. "Ye should nae have done it. Made those accusations in public. Ye knew they would react in some sort of way."

By the man's breathlessness, he'd obviously run to help after someone had alerted him of what happened. "Go home lass."

"I-I cannot." Esme found it impossible to stand upright. "C-cannot b-breathe…"

"I will help ye." The man wrapped his arm around Esme's waist and together they slowly made it to her cottage. Once inside, she noted that Mege sat by the window. The old woman's face lit up at seeing them.

"Nice to have a visitor," Mege said, not seeming to notice that Esme was yet unable to straighten.

"Mege, I am Colin. Do ye remember me?"

"Aye," Mege replied with a toothless grin. "Are ye here to court my Esme?"

"No," Esme managed to say. "Colin is already married."

"Och," Mege said. "Such a good man."

The man gave Esme a knowing look. "Ye should keep away from the village for a few days. Those two will not stop doing things to scare others from making any public accusations."

Esme nodded. "Thank ye."

"What did ye do?" Mege asked, seeming to have a moment of clarity.

"Nothing to be worried about." Esme inched to the table and slowly lowered to a chair.

The breeze whirled in through the open window, bringing with it the scent of rain and nature.

As she sat and breathed in the scents, the pain in her stomach eased and she remembered her lost baskets. What would she feed Mege? It would have to be a cup of goat's milk because when she lost her baskets, she lost the food she'd purchased as well.

AFTER A FITFUL night of little sleep, Esme got up early the next day. A groggy Laith agreed to remain inside and care for Mege.

She hurried to the path in the forest that would lead to the creek and then across to where she could spy the Ross camp without being seen. It was probably wishful thinking on her part since they'd discovered her there and were probably keeping a close eye on the area.

More fearful of her own people, she didn't care if they found her. It was imperative that she get help from the Ross. If nothing else to save Laith from what would happen when Tavon decided to return and make her pay for humiliating him in public.

The day was as dreary as she felt, and she was glad for it. The steady rainfall gave her a bit more cover as she pulled the cloak that Erik had given her over her head and made her way into the cover of the dense woods. Once there, the rain did not penetrate as much, and she lowered the cloak to her shoulders.

Upon arriving at the creek's edge, she was immediately spotted by four horsemen on the opposite side. One raised an arm to get her attention.

"Remain there," he said and guided his horse across the creek.

The man was huge and intimidating. A battle ax hung from the horse's saddle and a huge shield was slung across his back. The man's gaze met hers, the flatness sent shivers of fear through her.

"What are ye doing?"

"I-I must speak to Erik. It is a matter of life and death. P-please." She looked over her shoulder, scanning the ground and then up to the branches. "There," Esme pointed toward Hamish's land. "There is an abandoned shed. Tell him I will be waiting. He must come. I must save my brother."

"How do I know ye are not leading him to a trap?" The man had yet to look away, his gaze piercing.

"Ye can see it clearly from here. No one can approach

without ye noticing. I must save my brother. He must be kept safe."

The man shook his head. "If he decides to meet with ye. Ensure ye are alone. He will decide where ye are to bring yer brother."

Esme nodded and then hurried away. Ensuring not to be seen, she stayed as close to the edge of the woods as possible before darting to the empty dilapidated shed.

Despite the holes in the walls, Esme was not as cold as she expected mostly because of the thick cloak she wore. It was amazing what earning proper coin could provide for a person, she considered ruefully. When Laith left to live with clan Ross he would be able to afford such things, she was sure of it.

Having carefully arranged a stack of branches to keep off the damp ground, Esme must have fallen asleep because when the door opened and Erik stepped inside, she sat up with a start.

Looking like a Viking from the high seas with wind-tussled hair and a fur-lined cloak, Erik's blue gaze took in every inch of the shed before meeting her gaze. "What is it that ye truly seek?"

CHAPTER EIGHT

EVEN THE THREAT of death could not have kept him away from the beauty who looked up at him now as if he was the mightiest man in the world. Her hair had come loose from the braid and curls framed her face in a tangle of dark auburn silken tresses.

"Thank ye. In truth, I was not sure ye would come," Esme said remaining atop the rather lopsided cot she'd built. "I must beg for yer help." With care not to fall, she stood. It was then he noted she wore his other cloak.

His thoughts floated into territory he'd successfully avoided, until now. For a moment, she appeared before him wholly naked, laying over his cloak. The pink tips of her breasts beckoning his mouth, the area between her legs glistening with her need for him.

Erik cleared his throat and looked past her at a hole in the wall. "The man ye spoke to, Balgair, said ye wished for help for yer brother."

"Aye." She moved closer, and Erik almost took a step back. The wench had put a spell on him, he was sure of it. "My brother is in danger. I must get him away from the village."

At noting a bruise on her cheek he leaned in closer to inspect it. Her breath caught at his nearness. "Did someone hit ye?"

Esme shook her head. "Nay. I do laborious work and sometimes branches or such scratch my face."

He wondered if she told the truth.

"Ye seemed fearful of the council. Did they harm ye in any way?"

Again she motioned negatively. "I do not wish to speak of them. What I summoned ye for was to ask that ye help my brother. If he can leave and work for ye, then when the time is right I will follow."

"Where do ye plan to go?" He realized his voice sounded breathless. The close proximity to the beauty affected him like no other had in a very long time.

"I will go wherever Laith decides. We will find work."

Her gaze fell to his lips, and she let out a breath. "Why do I feel as if we have known each other before?"

The question took him by surprise. He'd felt the same way. "I am sure we have never met."

She dropped her gaze to the ground. "I have wondered what it would be like to be kissed by ye again."

As his mouth crashed over hers, she clung to him, kissing him back. It was desperate, savage and at the same time unbelievably enthralling.

Esme clung to him and unable to stop, Erik kissed her again, this time with as much gentleness as he could muster.

Their breaths hitched and they clung to one another. Erik's entire being clamored for more to happen, but he would not allow it. Despite what the man had called her, to him it was obvious she was innocent by the inexperienced way she returned his kisses and the way she seemed to trust him.

When she lifted her gaze to him, there was moistness in

the dark pools. "I have never been kissed like this before," she whispered. "It is lovely."

Air expanded his chest at the pride he felt at her words. "Ye are lovely."

Esme proffered her mouth up to him and without hesitation, he took it. His arms surrounded her body, bringing her against him in a tight embrace. She fit so perfectly. Seeming to meld into just the right places. Despite himself, he pressed his hardened sex into her, and Esme gasped. Then she deepened the kiss, her fingers threading through his hair, her plush breasts flush against his chest.

If it continued, he would not be able to keep from having her. Erik broke the kiss and then pressed his lips to the side of her face.

Her breathing was ragged as she clung to him with the desperation of a person afraid they may drown. "I-I will never forget this," she whispered and kissed the side of his neck. "Never."

"Tell me the truth, Esme. What happens in yer village? I wish to help."

There was sadness in her expression. "I do not believe there is anything that can be done. The council rules the village. The people are scared of them. They think it's safer to just stay out of the way than to fight for freedom."

"There are more of ye, than those in the council." Erik pushed a strand from her cheek. "The people can stand together against them. Or ye can always leave."

"I only care about my brother. I must remain to care for Mege. She is too frail to travel."

"I will help yer brother."

A look of relief spread across her face. She took a deep breath. "Truly?" Lifting the cloak that had fallen off her shoulders, she pulled it around herself.

"Aye." Already the distance between them made him want to reach for her anew. But it would be a bad idea.

Her cheeks pinkened when she met his gaze. "I will send my brother to ye tomorrow."

"What of ye?" Erik asked. "What will happen to ye?"

"Honestly, I am not sure."

"Ye can come with yer brother. Both leave."

She looked at him, her lips curving into a sad smile. "I cannot leave old Mege. She sacrificed her life for us. I must remain with her."

When she tried to round him, Erik took her arm. "What is yer true reason to remain? What are ye not saying?"

She shivered but was silent.

"Tell me," Erik insisted.

Esme shrugged. "It is only Mege. I cannot leave until she leaves this world."

She reached for the door and lifted her gaze to him. For a long moment she studied his face, then let out a sigh. "It was him. The man ye saved. The one who fell from the tree. He killed the man and injured the wee lass. The council will never do anything about it."

With another prolonged look, Esme left, and Erik had never before felt so conflicted.

In the depths of his being, he knew Esme had been truthful and feared for her brother's safety. She'd been desperate to be close to someone and feel safe, wanted, assured.

Hopefully he'd done that.

The door opened and Balgair peered in. "What did she want?"

"For her brother to leave Creag. I suspect she and him are in danger."

Balgair looked him over as if expecting to find a dagger protruding from his chest.

"Do ye remember the man who fell from the tree? She says it was he that killed the man that we found in the woods with the wee lass. We must catch the bastards in the act." He stalked out from the shed. "Burn it down."

"They will be alerted we were here," Balgair stated, his gaze taking him in. "Are ye sure?"

"Aye. I want them to know."

The flames of the shed rose quickly, and riders appeared several moments later from the direction of Creag.

Erik did not see the one he looked for. When the riders came closer, he and his men did not move.

"Ye came on our lands! Set a fire!" one of the men shouted.

"Tis a reason to kill every one of ye," said another.

Balgair held his battle ax over his head. "Ye and yers do nowt unless there are defenseless people alone."

The men grumbled turning to each other as if unsure how to respond. Finally the first one did. "Come again and ye will find trouble."

"I'm tremblin'," Balgair replied. The Ross warriors laughed.

"Ye should be," another of the men from Creag called out and spit on the ground. Then they rode away. Erik tracked their movements noting they did not ride toward the village, but directly across to the other border with Ross lands.

"Ensure our men patrolling in that area are aware," Erik instructed a scout who took off at a gallop.

ONCE BACK AT camp, Erik met with Torac to inform him of all that occurred. He left the part of what actually occurred between him and Esme out of the conversation. Like Balgair—who'd given him uncertain looks the entire way back to camp—Torac would also think him daft for having succumbed. True the wench could be using him in an effort to bring his guard down, but he sincerely doubted it.

"Struan is here," Torac said referring to their friend who'd remained behind on the northwestern shore. "With him is a healer by the name of Graeme."

"A healer?" Erik stood from the table and left their newly built guardhouse and headed to the larger warriors' quarters. There they found Struan and a man Erik assumed was the healer standing over a man moaning in pain.

"What happened?" Erik asked as he neared and looked to the man on the cot. It was one of the archers; a young man whose name he could not recall.

"His horse got spooked. It dropped him and one of its hooves crushed his leg." Struan frowned. "Looks bad."

With Struan and another man's help to keep the archer still, the healer held the leg in place with wood on two sides and began wrapping it. The poor man could not keep from yelling out in pain at each subtle move.

"Graeme," Struan said motioning to the healer with his head. Then looking to the healer and motioning to Erik he said, "The leader of the guard, Erik."

"Welcome," Erik said and walked away to find a volunteer

to take a message to the laird and let him know that they would have to attack the village to get rid of the men responsible for the attacks and killings.

EACH TIME LAITH looked to her, Esme could feel her face turn hot. He, of course, didn't know what she'd done, but she felt as if it was written all over her face.

Just thinking of Erik made her stomach tighten, and her breath catch. Kissing with him had been the most beautiful moment of her miserable existence. She was sure she'd never know such passion again.

"Ye have not heard a word I said," Laith commented, his gaze on her. "What happens?"

Her brother was so young and deserved a better life than to be mistreated by people in the village. "I spoke to Erik, the leader of the Clan Ross warriors. He agreed to take ye on as an apprentice. To work with the horses."

It was only for a moment, but Laith's face brightened, with a look of disbelief and joy. Then seeming to understand she left something out, he frowned. "Will he also help ye and Mege?"

"We will come later. First ye must go. I will say that ye left to go sell my baskets at Taernsby."

Laith gave her a dubious look. "That will only give ye a few days, perhaps three or four at most. What do ye plan to do"— he turned to glance at Mege who slept restlessly—"about her? She cannot travel."

"I will wait until I can join ye. It will not be long." Esme wiped an errant tear from her face. "It is imperative that ye go now as ye have work. I promise to follow as soon as I can. It will be easier if I go alone once it is time."

"No. I will remain here with ye. We go together."

"The leader will find someone else to do the work. Ye have to go. We require ye to earn a living once we leave here. Please, Laith."

It took a bit more convincing before Laith finally agreed to go the next day.

"Go at dawn by the path I showed ye. Ensure no one sees ye."

There was no sleep to be had that night. Mege became ill. Her breathing ragged and her face hot.

Esme placed wet rags on her brow, replacing them often in an effort to cool her down. While she sat there changing the cloths, she kept thinking of Erik. The soft press of his lips. The strength when he embraced her. Mostly she thought of how his eyes had darkened to a stormy blue as he'd made her feel like the only woman in the world. For those few moments, it was as if no one else existed.

When Mege finally settled, Esme climbed onto the bed and prayed the old woman would live until dawn.

Upon waking, Esme immediately felt Mege's face. She was cooler and seemed to be sleeping comfortably.

The worry over Mege subsided and she sat up only to inhale sharply at noting that Laith had already left.

She covered her face and cried while praying that he arrived at the camp unharmed.

WET AND SHIVERING, a young man walked toward camp with a sodden sack over his shoulder. When he neared, Erik recalled him from the first day he'd arrived. Besides, the resemblance left no mistake that it was Esme's brother. The lad was older than his years by the worry lines across his forehead and lack of fear at approaching a warrior.

"Why am I really here?" he asked Erik. "Esme said that I should come, that ye have work for me, and she would come later. I do not believe her."

Erik met the lad's gaze, unsure of what to say that would not send him back to the village. He decided to tell him the truth. "Yer life is in danger. She is ensuring ye are not harmed."

"What about her?" he asked looking over his shoulder. "She claims to have a plan but made me promise to come here first."

To that Erik had no reply. "She did not tell me more than ye. I have work for ye and can provide shelter and food. I am sure she will come as soon as she is able."

"Do ye do that for everyone?" Laith's eyes narrowed with suspicion.

Erik should his head. "No."

Seeming to know Erik would not expand, the boy didn't ask any other questions.

When Balgair walked up, his gaze fell on Laith before looking to Erik. "Come boy, I will show ye where ye will sleep and which horses ye will be responsible for."

The slight lad looked even smaller as he walked alongside the huge warrior toward the door into the guard's quarters.

If nothing else, he had to admire Esme's loyalty to her

brother.

Just then the scout he'd sent to warn the Clan Ross warriors about the riders, headed toward the camp. Erik walked to where the man slowed and dismounted.

"What happened?"

"The riders from the village did not go farther than their own lands. The Ross warriors are patrolling the area and will be keeping an eye on the border.

It was good to hear that Clan Ross was alert and ensuring the borders were secure. If only he could do the same for the forest. The villagers needed to go into the woods to hunt and find food.

"Have there been any more attacks by the encroachers?"

The scout shook his head. "Seems they have gone into hiding."

"Get food and rest," Erik instructed the man and went to seek out Torac.

The next morning, Erik spoke to Torac and Struan over first meal.

"From today forth, we will concentrate our patrols in the forest, in small groups that stay as close to the creek as possible. It is our land, not theirs. They will be reminded."

"They know the land better, even on our side of the creek. Our men will be at a disadvantage," Torac rebutted. "I do not agree that we should send small groups. We should send a larger one."

It was time to assert himself. Erik would stand by his decision. "It is an order."

Moments later, the guardsmen were lined up and awaiting instructions. Erik motioned Torac to speak. The man gave him a pointed look and stepped forward.

"We will concentrate our patrols on the forest. Groups of three warriors and one archer will spread throughout to ensure there are no trespassers. Stay alert, keep each other safe."

Erik stepped forward. "Ensure to spread out. I want every inch of the forest patrolled."

The warriors looked to Torac as if expecting he would say something else. The man stood silent.

Once the men were assigned to groups—which would patrol during the daytime only—Erik decided that he too would ride out and patrol the edges of the forest.

Thoughts of Esme filled his mind. More than anything he wanted to go see her. Whoever the old woman was, it was a huge price to pay if Esme were forced to marry someone. She could have come with her brother and been given shelter. Surely the old woman she cared for could have traveled the short distance.

Perhaps she wished to marry and remain there in the village where she'd lived her entire life. Why then the desperate look of someone who had little choice in life?

Erik looked up to the gray sky hoping it would not rain again. The fur-lined tartan he wore was thick, but not heavy enough. Before winter, he'd have to acquire a heavier cloak, like the one he'd given to Esme.

Once again, the picture of her kiss swollen lips returned. He let out a long breath and guided the horse to a crest he'd ridden up on. There were duties to perform. He had men to lead and people to protect. This was not the time to act like a lovestruck lad over a woman who seemed to be out of reach.

CHAPTER NINE

E SME HURRIED BACK to the cottage with an armload of thin branches. Already a huge pot of water boiled where she'd submerge them to make them soft enough to weave into baskets. Everything that day was like those before. No one suspected or knew Laith was gone.

She thought of Erik and considered returning to the edge of the woods in hope of getting a glimpse of him.

He'd asked why she did not come with Laith and had not seemed to understand when she'd replied that it was due to caring for Mege. Of course, he had no concept of her life there in Creag or knowledge that the old woman would not survive alone.

Hopefully he did not think she'd allowed his attentions because she wanted his help. In truth, she'd wanted him since she had first laid eyes on him. Never in her life had she felt so drawn to a man. He was like the brightest star in the sky. Something to be looked upon and admired, but never touched. Everything about him was so beautiful and so out of reach.

After dropping the branches to the ground, she picked up a small ax and began removing any nubs, leaving them as clean as possible before sticking them into the hot water.

The heat from the fire helped keep her warm as a cool breeze blew through bringing with it smells of the earth and sea. The mixture so familiar and yet still astonishingly refreshing.

"Esme," Mege called from inside, her voice barely audible.

The old woman had tried to get up from the bed and had fallen onto the floor.

"Oh, no." Esme hurried to her and tried to lift her only for the feeble woman to cry out in pain.

"I will have to find someone who can lift ye," Esme said pulling a blanket over Mege. "I will return shortly. Try not to move."

She gave Mege a drink of warmed milk, placed a folded blanket under her head, and hurried toward the village.

Although Hamish was closer, the old man would not be able to help. She would fetch Colin, surely he would help her.

"Where are ye going in such a hurry?" Tavon came upon her on a horse. "Looking for me?"

Deciding that although the man scared her, he would easily be able to help. "Mege fell. I require help lifting her from the floor. Will ye?"

Tavon studied her for a moment, his half-closed eyes revealing nothing. "Aye, fine."

She raced back to the cottage, not caring to ride with Tavon, and hurried through the door. He entered a moment later and peered down at Mege.

"Be with care," Esme said moving away from Mege, who was silent.

"Is she dead?" Tavon lifted the slight woman and placed her on Laith's cot. "She looks dead. Did ye kill her?"

"She is not dead," Esme said moving closer. Mege was strangely quiet making Esme's breath catch. "Mege?" She reached and touched the woman's shoulder. "Mege!"

When Esme began sobbing, Tavon dragged her out the front door kicking and screaming. "Ye cannot do anything now. She is gone."

"She cannot be gone." Esme tried to run back inside unsure why the brute did not allow her to. "Let me go!"

"Ye can stay with me," Tavon said into her ear. "No need to go back in there. Yer brother can bury her."

"No! Laith and I will ensure a proper burial. Leave me be." Esme stomped on his foot. Tavon cursed and slackened his hold on her. Esme yanked herself free and ran back inside, slammed the door shut, and barred it.

Esme remained frozen, her back against the door. Afraid that if she neared Mege, it would confirm she was dead. By the lack of sounds outside, Tavon had gone. She went to the window and peered out to confirm it.

Esme walked to where poor Mege looked to be sleeping and she crumpled to the floor, sobs erupting from her in bursts. Her chest threatened to explode with the pain and lack of breath.

Although it was eminent, Esme was not prepared for how agonizing it was to lose the woman who'd taken both she and her brother in as foundlings and cared for them despite her poverty.

Knowing she had to act, Esme trudged out and walked past the boiling water, ignoring it. Esme did not have the energy to do much more than pull Erik's cloak tightly around her shoulders and head to Hamish's house. She would ask for help burying Mege. Hopefully he would send for his son.

Halfway to Hamish's cottage the scent of smoke made her

sniff the air. Her eyes rounded and she whirled around.

"No!" Esme screamed at the horrible sight of her cottage engulfed in flames. She raced back as fast as she could, her feet felt like stones the faster she tried to run.

When she finally arrived, the entire front of the cottage was on fire. "No, no, no." Esme went to the back entrance. She had to get her coin. What little she had was all inside.

When she pulled the back door open, smoke billowed out. Her vision blurred. There was no choice, she had to go inside and get to the box that held the money.

Flames lapped out like fiery tongues, and she fell backward onto the ground.

WHEN SHE OPENED her eyes, it was dark outside, she lay on the ground staring at the starlit sky and couldn't figure out why someone kept shaking her.

At once recalling that the cottage had burned, she sat up and realized she was in front of what was now a pile of ashes. People meandered about, some shaking their heads, others looking to one another and speaking in low tones.

"We heard about Mege," Lattie said. At the sound of her friend's voice, Esme turned and saw that Lattie sat on the ground next to her, while her husband stood nearby looking on.

Confused, Esme looked to her friend. "What happened?"

"Yer cottage burned to the ground. Ian and I came running hoping ye were not inside. We didnae find ye for a long time. Someone happened upon ye behind the cottage on the ground and carried ye here."

"My coins!" Esme had run to the back, hoping to get in. It

was futile. The sack that contained the coin she'd been so carefully saving was gone.

"Oh, no." She wrapped her arms around herself and rocked as tears ran down her face.

As the mixture of ash and tears plopped onto her dirty arms she'd never felt so low, so lost.

"I give up," she muttered over and over. "I do not wish to continue."

"Shh," Lattie said rubbing Esme's shoulder. "Come on, there is nae much that can be done here. Come to our house."

A man came rushing toward her. "Where is Laith? Was yer brother inside?"

It was the perfect opportunity to ensure no one went after him. The look of astonishment on her face must have been convincing because everyone who stood near went silent.

Esme fell over to the ground. It was an act, but at the same time she could not withstand any more as all strength left her.

"IT IS BEST that ye marry to have protection. Ye must as ye have nowhere to live." Rafe stood just outside Lattie's front door managing to look down his nose at Esme who sat on the porch. It had been only a few days since the cottage burned and Mege had died. Why was the man there pestering her?

She wore one of Lattie's discarded shifts that was too wide and too long. After tearing a strip of fabric from the hem, she'd used it as a belt to keep the garment from falling off of her.

Someone had gifted her a shawl and shoes, for which she

was grateful. She'd asked Lattie to put away Erik's soot-stained cloak as she didn't wish to get questioned about it.

"I will ask Hamish. I am sure he will allow me to live in the abandoned shed near his home."

Rafe shook his head. "It was burned down as well. Probably by the same person who burned yer home."

Esme remained silent. It was the fire she'd left unattended when she ran to fetch Hamish that had burned down her house. However, the shed . . . that made no sense.

"I do not wish to marry anyone."

"Tavon has volunteered. Ye have little say in the matter. Ye are without family to speak for ye." The man turned on his heel and walked away.

The sound of a wailing bairn came from inside along with the voice of Lattie's mother-in-law trying to soothe him.

"I will take him out," Esme said as she walked inside and took the child from the cradle as the older woman looked on. It was clear Ian's mother didn't care for Esme being there, she'd not spoken a word to her since her arrival two days earlier.

Now as she walked out with the crying child, the woman turned away and went to the kitchen.

Lattie and Ian's house was not large, but the cottage had enough room for their family of seven—including Ian's mother. Despite this, Esme could tell she did take away from what little free space there was.

Once outside the child quieted and looked about with interest at the branches of the tree Esme walked to.

"See, no need to fuss wee one," she whispered pressing a kiss to the downy soft hair on the bairn's head.

She looked toward the village and considered her options. They would not give her a choice in whether or not to marry Tavon. The choice was already made by the council.

There was little doubt in her mind that if she did marry him her life would be a horrible one. As it was, the way he treated her was terrifying. Esme could not imagine the things he would do if she was bound to him.

As soon as darkness fell, she would leave. There was no other option than to run.

"Ye look so sad," Lattie said as they cleared off the remnants of the meal that evening. Her friend had returned from the market and informed Esme that they would work together to make baskets so that Esme could earn coin and support herself.

Esme had admitted to Lattie that Laith was alive, and her friend understood why she'd allowed people to think he was dead.

As Lattie explained plans for Ian to build her a small cottage and she would gift her hens, the pretty picture made Esme want to sob. Her heart broke more with each word as the life Lattie described was never to be.

"Ye are such a good friend." Esme wiped away tears. "However, I must leave," she whispered and then told Lattie what Rafe had said.

Lattie huffed. "They have nothing better to do than to pry into people's lives. Ye should get to choose who to marry."

"I agree, but ye know I will not be given the choice. I prefer to leave."

"Where?" Lattie whispered. "Ye have no one. Do not know anyone."

Esme stared out the window. "Aye. I know. Perhaps I will ask the man from Clan Ross camp to take me to Taernsby. Tavon will try to find me if I remain close, as he will not take my rejection well."

Just then there were knocks on the door and they heard Ian speak to a man. Chills ran down Esme's spine. Surely Tavon did not come for her now. It was late.

"He wants to talk to ye," Ian told her, his expression dark. "I will watch from the door."

Esme grabbed her shawl. "Do not do anything. I do not want to cause ye any more problems."

As she walked to the door, Ian's mother came from the back. "Ye should go. Ye'll cause my son trouble."

Outside Tavon stood next to his horse. He looked her over, his eyes hesitating at her waist and the crooked hem of her shift.

"What is it?" Esme said not going too close. "What do ye want? It is late."

He shrugged and rolled his eyes. "What does it matter? I am to be yer husband; I need no reason to see ye."

"We can speak tomorrow…" Esme took a step backward when he stalked toward her.

He grabbed her arm roughly and pulled her to the horse. "I say we talk now."

They rode for a short distance to the edge of the trees, past the shed where she and Erik had been together. She stared at the burnt pile of wood and pictured what it would be like to belong to a man who actually cared for her.

She had little doubt what Tavon planned to do. That he did not wait until they were properly married told of how little regard the man had for her.

"I want to go back," she protested. "It is cold."

"Shut yer mouth. I cannot stand a mewling woman."

She bit her bottom lip to keep from telling him how much she hated him. Instead, she looked straight ahead. If he tried to take her by force, she would fight him.

They reached an area where she could hear the creek water trickling past. It was obvious that Tavon had brought others there. He dismounted and yanked her from the horse.

From between two trees, he yanked out a tattered blanket.

"Take yer clothes off."

"I will not," Esme said crossing her arms. "It is cold, and we are not married. Ye took me once by force, I will not allow it again."

The hard slap sent her staggering sideways. Fear curled in her stomach, Esme bent and grabbed a rock, and she turned to face him. "Take me back to Lattie's. Let me go. Please."

When she threw the rock, it missed Tavon, but hit his horse, the startled animal took off.

Tavon stared after it. "Ye always make everything difficult."

He grabbed her arms and pulled her forward. "Ye like it rough. Prefer to be beaten into submission. Is that it?" The words made her shake with fear.

"Stop it," she called out when he threw her onto the ground face first and began yanking at the bottom of her ill-fitting dress.

Kicking out at him, she landed a hit to his nose and his grip slackened. She scrambled away and tried to get to her feet, but Tavon was too fast. He grabbed her ankle and dragged her back. As she was pulled across the ground, she grabbed a stick hoping to knock his brains loose.

Tavon flipped her onto her back, but she continued to fight for all she was worth. She swung the stick wildly about as he dodged her blows. One slap had her knocked flat onto her back once again, but she wasn't giving up.

Tavon rushed forward; the tattered blanket twisted around his ankles. Unable to stop he fell like a mighty tree straight on top of Esme. She screamed out in pain. The stick had sliced her side and the pain was made worse by his weight.

"It hurts. Please get off me." She gasped out the words at the man who didn't stir. Slowly the realization of what had occurred sunk in, and Esme struggled to push him away.

He'd been pierced as well.

It took several tries before she was finally able to shove him off of her and she crawled away to lean on a tree. The stick had cut her skin, but it had pierced Tavon. Straight through the chest.

Scared he'd come to and beat her; Esme rolled him over and stared down at him. The stick was protruding from his chest.

He groaned and Esme jumped backward.

"I am going to kill ye whore," he gasped out, seeming to have a hard time breathing.

Esme began crying. This was going to be it. How she died.

He wrapped his hands around the stick and tried to pull it out, but his hands fell away. "Take...i-it...ou..." His head lolled to the side.

"Oh, my, God. Forgive me." Esme fell to her knees unsure what to do. She had taken a life. She had killed a man.

They would find her, and she would hang.

Blindly she hurried away to the creek and washed her hands and face. There was blood on her dress, and she considered rinsing it, but there was no time.

It was best to escape. To run as far as possible before anyone found Tavon.

ESME RAN AND ran, pushing branches out of the way, tripping several times and falling on all fours before she scrambled back to her feet and continued on. Her lungs burned, each breath harder than the one before and still she continued on.

The further she went, the darker the forest became. Sheer terror filled her at the thought of coming across a predator. Slowing her progress as it became hard to see in the darkness, she finally collapsed next to a fallen tree.

As soon as she stopped, the cold dampness of the forest enveloped her, and she began to shiver.

A short bush gave some respite from the cold, and she curled up next to it to wait for morning.

AS SOON AS daylight broke, Esme looked herself over. The branch had not penetrated her side, only grazed it, so the wound did not bleed. Her dress was bloodstained, and she wondered what to do about it. Her skirts were grimy and torn, her hair a tangled mess, and in the struggle she'd lost her shawl.

She was a fright. It would be impossible to approach someone without eliciting questions.

At hearing voices, she hid and peered from behind a tree as a fisherman walked toward the shoreline. Esme tracked him for a bit and then looked to his cottage. Just then the front door opened, and a woman went around to the side. She carried feed for the chickens and began spreading it.

As fast as she could Esme rushed to the small home and went inside. Once there, she blindly grabbed clothes and hurried back out.

Holding the bundle, Esme continued forth, following the shoreline that led away from her village and in the direction the sun had risen.

When she found a berry bush, she stopped to pick berries and eat, while keeping an eye out for animals that would be looking for a meal as well.

The clothes she'd taken had turned out to be a skirt and a shawl, but no blouse. She pulled the skirt on over her current tattered one and wrapped the shawl around her shoulders. The warmth almost made her cry.

There was nothing to be done, but to keep running.

CHAPTER TEN

I T WAS IMMEDIATELY evident something bad had happened, by the speed at which the warriors approached. They were his men, so Erik rushed forward to greet them.

All three men were bleeding. Some still had arrows protruding from their body. One was slumped over and fell from his horse hitting the ground with a sickening thud.

"They attacked us," one of the men, who had several arrows in his back said while being helped to dismount. "They claim we left one of their men for dead near the creek."

Graeme, the healer, hurriedly explained where the men should be carried. The one on the ground was left to last as he was already dead.

Following the injured men, Erik barked out questions.

"Where did this happen?"

"Who did it?"

The man who'd spoken went slack and the healer motioned for the men to bring him inside.

Erik hurried to another warrior. His eyes were glazed over from the pain. "Th-the same... ones..." He attempted to catch his breath.

"He cannot be made to talk," Graeme said shoving Erik away. "Let me try to save him."

Outside the guard quarters, Erik paced impatiently. How

could they have been caught by surprise? There were plenty of patrols out there to ensure it was safe.

MOMENTS LATER TORAC and his three companions came from the forest. Torac's tunic was bloody, and Erik wondered if he too had been struck.

By sundown, one man was dead, and several warriors were injured, some badly.

"It was stupid of us to go in there in small groups not knowing the territory as well as them," Torac yelled, his fury lashing out at Erik. "Ye should have expected this would happen."

"We cannot give in to a small village. We patrol again tomorrow."

"We?" Torac stalked forward until they were almost nose-to-nose. "I did not see ye out there."

Erik shoved the man away.

A FOGGY HAZE hung low in the trees the following morning as Erik mounted with the two men who'd been chosen to ride with him. The warriors were mostly silent as they strapped shields to their arms and joined their groups. Instead of threes, they were to ride in groups of four and five.

The six groups rode from the guardhouse toward the forest. Two to the west, two to the east, and two—including Erik—went to the center.

The thick foliage made it hard to navigate making progress excruciatingly slow. They took turns keeping watch up at the trees and behind, expecting to be attacked from above as the ones the day before had been.

As the day progressed it was obvious that no one was in the forest that day. The villagers who'd attacked had been smart enough to stay away. They would be expecting retaliation, which meant approaching the village was not a smart thing to do.

At the same time, they would not sit idly by and allow another attack to happen on Ross lands without retaliating.

At the sounds of raised voices and screams, he and his men went toward it. The nearest group to them had felled someone from a tree and were fighting five men. Evenly matched, the Ross warriors soon overtook the less experienced men.

Erik and his men yelled and urged their horses toward the fight, the villagers immediately ran away, those that could. Two lay on the ground, one obviously dead.

"THE LAIRD REQUIRES ye to come," a messenger greeted him when they returned to the camp.

"What is this about?" Erik asked. "This is not the time for me to leave." He motioned to the injured men being brought into the guardhouse.

By the messenger's droll look, there was no room for argument.

Erik let out a breath. "When?"

"I would suggest ye leave at daybreak."

"Just me?"

The man shrugged. "I gave ye the message. Ye are required to speak to our laird."

"Torac," Erik called out motioning for the man to come closer. "I am going to the keep. Do ye wish to come? Struan can lead in my stead."

The warrior met his gaze. "Why?"

"Our laird wishes to see me." Erik looked past the man to the warriors who'd been instructed to remain at the camp for the time being.

"I prefer to stay."

"I suggest the men stay out of the forest for now."

Torac met his gaze. "I agree."

THE RIDE WOULD take a day and a half—possibly a bit longer—as Erik had decided to ride by Taernsby and speak to the leader of the guard there and let them know what had occurred. It could be they would have to unite and attack the village.

The day proved to be a pleasant one. Unlike the days before, the sun was shining and there was barely a cloud in the sky. He kept a keen ear on the birdsong to ensure no one else was about. If not for the constant need to keep alert for a possible attack, he would have enjoyed the ride.

When he saw a woman walking unsteadily through the trees, at first Erik thought it to be an illusion. Then upon catching a second glance, he recognized her.

"Esme!" he called out urging his steed to a gallop. "Esme!"

The woman ran as if her life depended on it.

If it was Esme, she did not respond. If it was not, then he'd just scared a poor unsuspecting woman half to death.

It had to be her, there was too much of a resemblance.

It was easy to catch up with her since he was on horseback, and she was on foot. She whirled to face him, and he cringed at the state of her. Scratched cheeks. Filthy clothes. She looked as if she'd been dragged behind a wagon.

"What happened?" he asked dismounting. "Why are ye here?"

Esme hung her head. "I must go away. I have to hide. I-I killed Tavon. They will hang me."

"So it was ye," Erik said eliciting a wide-eyed look. "Yer people attacked my men, one is dead."

"Oh, no." Esme looked as if to crumple, so he took her by the shoulders and guided her to sit next to a tree. "Now yer people will wish to punish me as well. I should have allowed him to do what he wished and not fought back."

"No," Erik said. "Ye have every right to defend yerself. And he is not dead. The men who attacked said that he was *left for dead*."

She let out a breath and sagged. "It matters not. I must leave. Help me get to Taernsby. I must find a way to get away. Go to another isle."

"Ye do not have to go." Erik could not think of what to say or do. He wasn't prepared to lose her. He had hung on to the illusion that there would be more times between them. Once everything settled, he'd hoped to get to know Esme better.

"Take care of Laith, please. Mege is dead." Her voice was soft. "I have lost what little I had. The cottage burned to the ground. With it the wee bit of coin I had saved."

When she began crying, Erik lowered himself next to her and held her against him. "Esme do not cry. We will find a way for ye to be safe. I promise."

"Ye cannot promise me that. I cannot continue to put ye and others in danger. Once Tavon is able to speak, he will tell them what occurred. The council will want me to pay for it."

"Come." Erik helped her stand. They went to his horse

where he mounted and then helped her up.

She lay against him and fell into an exhausted sleep. Either that or she'd given up fighting. All her strength and will—gone. The lass had been through so much. He wanted to protect her, to give her safety and security. More than anything, he wanted to be the one to do something to set things right. He made a silent promise to shelter her from danger and any further pain.

When they stopped to allow the horse to drink from a shallow pond, Erik helped Esme down.

They walked along the water, both bending to take a drink and rinse their faces and hands. Esme looked at him with curiosity. "Is this what ye do? Help those in distress?"

"Aye, I suppose that is my work." He reached for her hand. "Ye should nae worry. They will nae dare to come onto our lands to come after ye."

Her gaze moved from him to the direction of Creag. "I hope not. I am glad my brother is with ye. It was good that he listened."

They walked in silence a bit longer, her hand still in his. "Esme, what would ye wish for if given a choice?" Erik wasn't sure why he asked the question, but he sincerely wanted to know what she was thinking.

"I would wish for a home of my own. One where I could tend to a garden and not have to worry every day about from where my meal will come." Her face softened. "Perhaps a pair of bairns and a hardworking husband, but that is too much to expect."

Perplexed, he studied her. "Ye should not limit yer dreams. Tis hard enough to live in the reality of what life is."

"Ye are wise," she said, her lips curving and ever so entic-ing. "I supposed to expect little, leaves less room for disappointment."

"Come let us continue on our way. There is much to do." Erik said, but then held her back. "May I kiss ye Esme?"

Her eyes rounded, but then she nodded. A light blush stained her cheeks. "I would like it very much if ye did."

Pulling her closer, he leaned forward and pressed his lips over hers. Esme closed her eyes and let out a soft sigh upon him straightening. In truth, he had to pull away lest he continue forth and ask her to spend the night in a warm nest he'd make for them.

It was a bit later that they arrived in Taernsby. Instead of finding the leader of the guard, he went to the tavern and asked for a room and a bathing tub be brought.

While Esme bathed, he went to find a seamstress and pur-chased clothes for her. The woman looked him up and down. "I remember ye. Yer a guardsman who used to live here."

Erik nodded. "Aye, I am. I need clothes for a woman."

The seamstress gave him a questioning look and then rounded him to the doorway. "Is she with ye?"

He shook his head. "I require whatever it is a woman would need for a pair of days."

After some awkward motioning and guessing, when asked about Esme's size, he left the shop with two skirts and a bundle of other items including a pair of used shoes the woman was hesitant to sell him.

Esme was wrapped in a blanket asleep on the bed when he walked in. She looked too peaceful to bother, so he left the clothes and went downstairs.

A guard that he recalled was named Quinn entered when Erik was eating and walked to the table. "I heard ye came. Any news?"

Erik motioned for the man to sit. The tavern owner placed a tankard of ale in front of Quinn.

"There were some attacks. One of my men was killed, and several injured. They blame us for an attack on a man." Erik shrugged. "Strange they become so angered after one attack on one of their men, when someone has been killing our people for months. Yet they still want us to believe it's not them."

The warrior's gaze was flat. "That village is a nuisance. We should just take it over."

"I am on my way to see our laird. Hope to convince him to do just that." Erik let out a breath. "How are things with the encroachers?"

"We believe they are in hiding—waiting. Not sure what for. Perhaps their leader was wounded or killed and now they find themselves without a plan as to what to do next."

It sounded as if Quinn and his men had peace, at least for the time being, which was helpful in case Laird Ross gave the order for them to go to battle against Creag.

"I am sure our laird will send a message if we require some of yer men to help us."

"Who is the woman?" Quinn's question caught Erik by surprise. Although it shouldn't have, obviously the warrior had lookouts to make sure they were not caught off guard in case the encroachers returned.

"She is someone I rescued from the village. Her brother is apprenticing with us."

The warrior frowned. "Are ye sure they are not spies?"

"At first no, I was not. But after their cottage was burned to the ground and she had to flee for her life, it is obvious they are not."

"How long will ye remain?" Quinn asked.

"I leave in the morning."

They sat in companionable silence while Erik finished his meal. Looking up he noticed Esme enter the room. She stopped at seeing Quinn.

"Come," Erik said waving her over. Upon her approach, he introduced her to his companion.

"I best go," Quinn said. "If ye need a place, let me know," he added looking at Esme.

She lowered to the chair across from him, her gaze glued to his now empty bowl. "Can I bother ye for something to eat?" Her voice was barely above a whisper.

Erik pulled out a small purse, picked out ten coins, and handed them to her.

"I cannot accept—"

"I must leave ye here. How else do ye plan to pay for a place to live and for food and such until I return for ye?"

Just then the serving woman brought a bowl of steaming stew and fresh bread. She slid the bowl in front of Esme and smiled. "Ale or cider?"

"Cider, please," Esme replied and looked to Erik. "Ye had already told them I would wish to eat?"

Erik nodded. "I spoke to the seamstress, she is called Flora, from whom I purchased the clothes ye are wearing, and asked about a place for ye to stay. She's agreed to ye living in a room above her shop. The room will be ready in the morning, she is clearing it out now. She lives right next door, so ye will be safe."

In between bites, Esme wiped away tears. "I do not know

what I would have done had ye not found me. I was praying for an answer."

"And I appear, the handsome prince on a steed. Rescuing the beautiful damsel in distress."

His comment elicited a shy smile. "Ye are certainly rescuing me. Why? Is it because ye and I kissed?"

"Nay, not only because of that," he said abruptly. "It is because ye matter to me."

Her eyes widened, but she said nothing. "Where are ye going?"

"I am on my way to see Laird Ross. He has requested to speak to me. I must ride at the break of dawn. Tonight we will stay here."

She nodded. "Can ye take me to meet the seamstress?"

Erik had to admit feeling proud at the admiring glances Esme garnered from men as they walked through the village. Despite the scratches on her face and ill-fitting dress, her beauty remained unmarred. The small pert nose, pouty lips, and large eyes were enticing. Esme's slight figure and large breasts were what most men dreamed of at night.

When a rather large man walked too close, she shrunk away and walked closer to Erik, her body pressed against his side. He could not imagine what she'd endured all these years with no protection of a family. The only one to count on was a much younger brother. No wonder the boy seemed so troubled.

At meeting the seamstress—a woman of about thirty. called Flora, the two women were immediately warm to one another, especially when Esme complimented her work and choices.

Erik stepped outside as they talked about what Esme could

expect and looked up at the sky. It continued to be a clear day and he hoped the next day would be the same as he traveled to see the laird.

Once he escorted Esme to the market to purchase whatever she needed, they would return to the tavern. He knew she would think he expected her to give herself to him, but he did not. However, he desired it more than anything. It would be a herculean task to keep from her. But he would not break the trust she had in him. Esme deserved to be treated well and given a choice in such matters.

When she emerged, she had a basket on her arm.

"Ye borrowed it?" Erik asked.

"Nay, she gifted it to me. I told her I made baskets, and she thinks I could sell them here at the market and make good coin."

His lips curved. "Ye are admirable, Esme. Truly admirable."

She beamed with pride. "I will repay ye. Do ye think Laith should come here and live with me?"

"Ye should not remain alone," Erik responded, wishing to add that he could be her protector. A part of him rebelled at the thought of a wife. His nomadic warrior's life did not allow for it. At the same time, something about this woman made him want to push away any thought that included a future without her.

"Come let us go to the market and then return to the tavern."

They walked to a few stalls, Esme purchasing very little even when he encouraged her to get more. Finally, he gave up and grabbed a few items that he figured she'd require and paid for them.

When they returned to the room in the tavern, Esme sat in a chair in front of the hearth and sighed. "I am not sure how to feel. I am relieved to be here, but also horribly worried about Laith and what he will face if caught by the village council."

"He is safe, no one can get to him while surrounded by my men."

She studied him for a long moment. "Is it wrong of me to feel relieved to be away from there and on my own? I want to do nothing more than sleep for days and not think about my every move."

He went to her and placing his fingers under her chin, he lifted her face up so he could look into her eyes. "Ye deserve to rest Esme. Has there ever been a time when ye did not have to worry about others?"

She closed her eyes and shook her head. "Never."

"I will leave ye to rest then. I must see about my steed as I have to leave at first light. I will return when it is time to eat."

Not waiting for her to reply, he hurried from the room ensuring the door was closed firmly before heading down the stairs. What he really wanted to do was ride out and ensure no one had followed them. He'd ask her to remain indoors for a few days until it is safe to go out just in case someone from her village had seen them.

He doubted someone from the village could get past the Ross guards without being questioned, but one never knew. There were many who traveled from the western side of the isle to Taernsby to trade products or visit family. Someone from Esme's village could easily blend in without it being obvious they are not Clan Ross.

CHAPTER ELEVEN

E SME WOKE WITH a start at the sound of male voices. Whoever it was laughed jovially as they walked past the door. There was little light in the room; it was obviously late in the day. She must have slept for hours, and Erik had yet to return. At least he'd not come in and woken her.

Slipping from the bed, she went to the window and pushed the shutters open to peer out.

From the second floor of the tavern, she had a clear view of the village square. Only a few people meandered about, most of whom seem to be heading home as it would soon be dark. When she noticed Erik, he was speaking to a man who looked to be a warrior. The two were of similar height and muscular build that came from continuous sword fighting and horseback riding. The pair made a handsome sight. Erik with his golden hair and the other warrior with hair as dark as midnight.

The men looked toward the tavern, and she moved to the side so they would not see her. Erik motioned to the building and the other man nodded. Obviously, he told the warrior about her and that she would remain there. From the small amount of time she'd known him, Esme suspected he arranged protection for her.

She looked over her shoulder at the bed and wondered if

he would join her that night. Butterflies took flight, her stomach tightening at the thought. Never before had she considered how wonderful intimacy with the right man could be. Not until Erik.

When she peered out again, he walked toward the tavern with long purposeful strides. Esme rushed to the basin to splash water on her face and then tidied up her hair with the new comb he'd purchased for her at the market.

Just a few moments later, he entered the room and immediately searched the space for her, his gaze meeting hers. "Did ye rest well?"

"I may have slept too long," Esme replied, not at all sure why her face had become hot. "Have ye rested at all?"

"I will sleep tonight," he said and used the same water in the basin to wash his hands and face, it felt intimate to be sharing the small space. It was usually reserved for married people to share a room, basin, and cloths.

"I must speak to ye about how to go forward once I am gone," he said lowering to the same chair she'd just been sitting in.

Esme sat on the bed. "I am listening."

"For a few days, it would be safer if ye remain indoors. I do not think ye are in any danger, but someone could have followed ye and saw us come here. If that is so, hopefully they will think ye are with me when I leave tomorrow."

"I understand. But I must get food and..." Esme started only to stop when he held up a finger. "The seamstress, Flora, will ensure ye have food for a few days. I spoke to a Clan Ross guard; his name is Gavin. He will let ye know when it is safe to be out. He is good friends with the seamstress, so him going there will not be suspicious."

The woman seemed a bit older than the warrior she'd seen Erik speaking to and Esme wondered what kind of a relationship they had. "Are they courting?"

Erik's brow creased. "He rescued her from the shipwreck and helped bury her husband. I do not think there is more than friendship."

"It matters not, I suppose," Esme said with a long sigh. "Is there anything else I should know about?"

"There is a large Clan Ross guard post here making Taernsby very safe. Come, I will show ye," he went to the window, and she joined him as he pointed out toward the seashore. "See the long building there?"

She had to lift up on her tiptoes and stand against him to peer out. "Aye, I see it." Her voice was breathless. "It is very large."

"Aye, many men are there." The warmth of his breath tickled her ear. "I was posted here for many months."

Esme turned to look at him but quickly turned away. They were so close their faces almost touched. "Did ye like it here?"

When he moved away, Esme was disappointed. Perhaps it was silly to think he had deep feelings for her. Upon saying she was important to him; she'd assumed it was in a romantic way. It could be it was that he cared for her as one human does for another.

"I would consider living in Taernsby. It is very peaceful, and the villagers are a jovial, kind people."

His answer surprised her. Esme half expected him to tell her he preferred to remain at the keep. In the laird's service.

AFTER EATING LAST meal, Esme was in the room alone. With the excuse of checking on his steed, Erik gave her privacy to prepare for bed. Among the things he'd purchased from the seamstress was a warm night shift. She wondered how much coin he'd spent to ensure she had all she needed.

The fabric fell from her shoulders to her ankles and Esme felt rich in that moment. She'd never owned something so nice. She slid her hands over the fabric, enjoying the feel of it against her skin.

Just then the sight of her scratched hands caught her attention, and she held them up. Her nails were ragged and broken from fighting, and she knew scratches still remained on her face. She had been delusional to think a man like Erik would be attracted to her. Especially in the current state of things.

It didn't matter. What was important was that she was safe and for the time being could rest and begin a new life.

When the door opened and Erik walked in, he looked as if he'd bathed. His hair was damp, and he wore different clothes.

He held a bundle of blankets in his arms and began to unfold them and prepare a place to sleep by the fire.

"What are ye doing?" Esme asked.

He gave her a glance, his gaze roaming over the nightgown. "I do not see the need to pay for another room. I will sleep here on the floor."

"Ye can use the bed," Esme said helping to fold one side of the blanket under so that it would be thicker and more comfortable. "Ye have a long ride ahead of ye in the morning. These blankets are softer than anything I am used to. I can sleep here on the floor for one night."

Stopping to scratch his newly shaved chin, he gave her a

quizzical look. "What kind of a man would allow a woman to sleep on the floor while he sleeps on a bed?"

Esme had to chuckle. "Ye sound like Laith. A tired man who has a long hard day ahead."

When they finished preparing the pallet, he sat on the blankets and removed his boots while Esme lowered to the chair. "How long will ye be gone?"

"I do not imagine more than a pair of days. I will return directly to the camp. This stop was not planned."

"Erik," Esme began. "Once things are safe, can ye tell my brother to come see me?"

"I will." He studied her. "If we go to war against yer village. Ye could return home after. There is no question who would win. Clan Ross is larger with more seasoned warriors."

"That place is no longer my home." Her mind went to Lattie and her family. "I hope the women and bairns will not be harmed."

"We are not savages. It is only the men who attacked our people that we are after."

"Aye, but many times, innocents are harmed."

"'Tis the way of war." Erik stretched out on his back, placing his hands behind his head. "This is very comfortable." His lips stretched into a smile and Esme fought not to ask to join him.

DARKNESS THREATENED TO swallow her whole. A weight over her made it hard to breathe. Then there were hands everywhere, all over her body. Hot breath fanned her face as she struggled to get free, but it was impossible. Tavon was not there in Taernsby. It had to be a dream.

Even the tears that streamed down the sides of her face were hot, almost unbearable.

Slowly the grip of the nightmare lessened and breathing became easier. A faint breeze blew over her as her eyelids fluttered open and Esme realized she had indeed been dreaming.

In the moonlight, she could see the outline of Erik's body. He slept on his side facing away from the fire, his soft snores making her feel safe and secure.

Unable to remain in bed for fear of the dream returning, she slipped from it and went to the window. The shutters were open to allow for air, so she leaned out and looked up at the sky.

The dark expanse was replete with stars; the splendor of it helped dispel the fear. That so much beauty could exist along with cruelty and evil, was something she'd never comprehended. The balance of nature, she supposed.

When she turned back to the room, she slid a look to the bed and then to where Erik lay. He should have taken the bed, or she would have gladly shared it. They each staying on their side.

Lowering slowly, she touched his shoulder.

"Erik?"

He murmured something in his sleep and her heart squeezed. From what she could see, he was comfortable and slept soundly. It was best to let him rest where he was.

After adding a log to the fire, Esme lowered to the palette. The warmth of the embers in the hearth meant she did not require a blanket. So she turned toward the fire, her back touching his, and allowed slumber to claim her.

THE TOUCH OF Erik's lips on her neck and his arms around her was the way she would love to wake every morning.

"Why are ye here when ye have a bed that is all yers?" he murmured into her ear. "Not that I will complain."

Reaching up, she touched his face. "I had a bad dream. Ye make me feel safe."

"Mmm." His hardness brushed against her bottom. His arousal sending a clear message of what his body wanted. It was what she wanted as well. As unversed as Esme was in lovemaking, she hoped to have him, to know what it was like to have intimacy with a man she desired.

She lifted her face and press it against his shoulder, her heart thundering in her chest. "I want ye, Erik."

He made a sound like that of a man torn. "Are ye certain?"

"Aye," Esme gathered the courage to look into his eyes. "Aye, very much so."

The callousness of his fingers against her skin as he pulled her nightgown off, sent tingles of awareness all over. They'd not started making love and already Esme was alight with desire.

Erik stood and pulled off his breeches, revealing his hardness. Her gaze traveled over his magnificent body, wishing to memorize every bit of it. If only he was to be hers always. It was a dream that she'd hold on to.

When he came over her, Esme almost cried at the thought of what was to come and that she may never be with him again after that day. However, nothing matter, however, more than that moment. She was to be totally his.

Their mouths clashed in a passionate kiss, while their hands explored the other's body. His muscled body was warm and hard and worthy of a slow exploration—which she did.

He kissed her face and neck and licked his way down to her breasts. Sucking one hard peak into his mouth and then the other, while his fingers found the hooded nub right above her sex. Her mind and body reacted as delicious tendrils of fire rushed up and down her limbs. The world fell away. Each response began and ended with the incredible things his mouth and hands were doing.

Erik's held her by the hips, holding her in place as he slid his staff up and down the center of her sex, teasing her mercilessly. Esme squirmed beneath him as she tried to force him into the position her body cried out for. He chuckled softly, his body not stopping, and she dug her fingernails into the firmness of his bottom.

"I need ye," Esme gasped when he rose back up and looked down at her. "Now. All of ye."

For a moment both were still, gazes locked and searching. "Why do ye want me?" Erik finally asked. "I am but a lowly guard, nothing special."

The question took her by surprise and her lips parted, but no sound came out. Finding her voice, Esme caressed his face. "Ye are so much more than a guard. Ye are my protector as well as the defender of anyone who cannot do so for themselves. That ye take notice of me makes me feel more special than I ever have in my life."

Seeming to think about what she said, he let out a long sigh. "I have never…" He stopped and pressed a kiss to her lips. "I have never felt so close to someone as I do when with ye."

That the strong beautiful man was so vulnerable in that

moment made Esme wrap her arms around his waist and kiss his jawline and neck. "I feel the same, Erik. I cannot think of what it will be like when ye leave today."

Once again his eyes met hers. "Will ye... will ye wait for me?"

Tears filled her eyes and Esme smiled up at him. "Aye, of course I will."

"Good. That is good." Erik pushed his face into her hair and his entire body softened.

Esme tapped his shoulder. "Ye are quite heavy."

"Oh... sorry." He lifted and smiled at her. "There is something we should finish."

Moments later, he was thrusting into her, their bodies colliding with force. The sounds of flesh against flesh mixing with their moans as they got closer and closer to release.

"I need more of ye," Erik said, and slid his hands under her thighs and lifted her legs over his shoulders.

The depth of his drives were overwhelming, and Esme pulled the corner of the blanket over her mouth to muffle her screams of pleasure.

The room spun around them and then everything vanished. As she was lost in swirls of lights like the stars in the night sky, a wonderful heat traveled from where they were joined down her legs.

"Erik!" Esme screamed as she gave in to the onslaught of her release.

"Ah!" Erik lowered her legs and held her hips with both hands, as he continued to drive into her now pliant body. His beautiful face was taut, mouth open as he gasped in each breath. She wrapped her legs around him and he began to shudder.

Erik rolled off of her and both lay staring up at the ceiling, breathing hard.

After a moment, he rolled to face her. "Did ye mean it?"

"Wh-what?" Esme fought to regain control of her trembling body.

He pulled her against him. The solid strength of his arms and hard body was like a shelter from any storm imaginable.

"What did ye ask?" Esme said pressing a kiss to his lips.

"Will ye wait for me? Once I get things settled with the village. I wish to come back for ye and bring ye back to Welland. If ye wish."

Esme's eyes rounded. "Truly? Is that what ye want?"

He nodded. "Aye, I would not have said it otherwise."

Esme pushed him to his back and lifted up to kiss him over and over. "Aye, I will wait for ye. Of course, I will."

AFTER BREAKING THEIR fast, Erik walked Esme to the seamstresses' shop. They climbed the stairs to the room she would be renting, and Esme was delighted to see it was spacious and bright, with two windows that allowed plenty of sunlight in.

There was a small wood-burning stove that would allow for heat, a narrow bed, and a washstand. On the floor was a woven rug and along the wall a table and chair.

"It is perfect," Esme said smiling brightly at the woman who beamed with pride.

"Gavin helped me. I had to move other pieces out, so if ye feel like ye need anything more, just let me know," Flora said.

"I do not require anything more," Esme said and meant it. "I will be very comfortable here."

The woman gave a nod and left the room to give them privacy.

It was awkward in a way because it was obvious that she and Erik were more than friends. However, in that moment, Esme didn't care. She fought to not cry and beg to go with him.

"Promise to be safe," Esme said reaching up to cup his jaw. "I will miss ye."

"It will not be long. Two days there and after two or three more, I will return to camp. Once things get settled, I will come to see ye."

The way he made it sound did settle her mind, but there were so many things that could go wrong. He could change his mind. The laird could demand he remain at the keep. Then there was the matter of the village council at Creag.

Tavon would want revenge and he would not rest until he found her.

"Wait a few days before venturing out. Then stay indoors as much as possible."

Esme nodded. "I will, I promise."

His arms wrapped around her, and she clung to him in a desperate attempt to keep him there just a bit longer.

They kissed and she met his gaze. "Be with care."

CHAPTER TWELVE

THE RIDE TO Ross Keep was relatively smooth. Erik stopped twice to allow his horse to drink and rest before continuing on. By the end of the second day, the huge fortress came into view and his steed, seeming to sense a warm stall and fresh oats, picked up its pace.

Guards waved at him as he approached since his blond hair made him recognizable. Erik called out greetings and rode through the huge thick wooden gates that were open.

The courtyard was abuzz with activity. Carts were being unloaded. Servants were rushing back and forth to the kitchen doors.

Lads hurried from the stables to get his horse asking about his day before leading the willing animal away. In the center of the courtyard next to the well, a group of women were gathered, all turning to look at him before returning to their conversation.

"Erik, what brings ye?" It was Ewan Ross, one of the laird's brothers who greeted him. "I did not expect to see ye."

"The laird sent for me."

"Ah." The hazel gaze met his. Ewan was the less stern of the brothers. The archer seeming to be in a constant good mood. Just then three children rushed toward them, and Ewan shrugged. "I must go. I was supposed to hide so they could search for me."

He ran away, the trio of children racing to catch him with squeals of delight.

Like the courtyard, the great room was also bustling with activity. People were seated at long tables, others stood in a queue waiting for the laird to call them forward.

At the front of the room in an armed chair sat The Lion, the laird of Clan Ross. His rich golden tresses rather disheveled as he kept running his fingers through it while speaking to two men who argued.

Finally, Darach stood to his full height and motioned for two guards to come near. At the laird's call the two men who argued went silent. The Ross motioned to the men who'd been arguing and now looked on with wary curiosity. "Take these two to the practice field. Give them a broadsword each. Let them fight to first blood and return with them once that is done."

The men shook their heads. "I know nothing of swordplay, my laird," one stated.

"I cannot possibly," the other added.

"Finally ye agree on something." Darach shrugged and waved the guards away. "If ye return with another petty disagreement I will order that ye fight to the death."

The men paled as they walked away with their heads hung low.

At noticing him, the laird motioned him toward his study. As Erik made his way there, he grabbed bread and a half-filled cup of ale.

Once in the laird's study, Darach and a tall warrior, who served as his first, entered moments later.

"What in the hell is happening down there? Why are my men dead and injured?" The laird's booming voice seemed to echo from the walls. "Am I to believe a group of untrained villagers were able to overcome seasoned warriors?"

Erik swallowed. "It was my mistake to send them out in small groups. The villagers shot arrows from the trees and the men were caught by surprise."

"Why groups of three? Why not the entire unit go and raid the forest?"

"With a large group, it is hard to get through without being in a single line, which is just as dangerous." Erik drew a map of the area on parchment as best he could while explaining the region, the thickness of the foliage, and the creek that marked the border between the lands.

The laird studied him and what he drew as Erik explained everything in full detail.

Once the explanation was over, the laird's gaze was steady. "Ye will return with ten additional archers. I want the matter solved. Not one more death or ye will be removed from command."

Although being reprimanded stung, Erik felt he deserved every bit of it. It was his fault and no one else's that those men had been killed and injured.

"Three Ross men were also killed during a clash with men who claim to be Clan Robertson," Erik told the laird.

"Stay another day, I wish to know more details of what happens down there." The laird looked to his first. "Ensure ten archers are prepared to ride to Welland. They are to remain for as long as needed."

The man walked out after giving Erik an understanding

glance.

Seeming to have relaxed somewhat, Darach stood. "Get some rest, Erik. Eat. I must return to the complaints that await." The laird touched his shoulder as he walked past. "Ye are a good warrior, however, leading is far harder than fighting is it not?"

"Aye, it is," Erik replied.

STILL STINGING FROM the reprimand, Erik joined the guards in the field to practice. It was something to do to pass the time. He had no belongings at the keep, all his possessions had been sold or given away when he'd left after accepting his first post in Taernsby. He had been going post to post ever since. Now he was to live in the southwest for an undetermined amount of time.

There were decisions to be made, especially since he now planned a future with Esme.

Blocking the downfall of a sword, Erik shoved his opponent away and swung only for his blow to also be blocked. His opponent smiled and before he knew what happened, he lay on his back, the wind knocked out of him.

"Ye are distracted." The man's face loomed over his. "Could mean death in battle."

Annoyed at the truth of the man's words, he jumped to his feet and went on the offensive until his opponent's sword went flying from his hand.

The man held both hands up. "Worthy show of skill. However, ye are dead, so it matters not," he said with a chuckle.

Erik couldn't help but laugh. "Aye, ye are right."

For the rest of the day, there wasn't anything much he

could do other than join the guardsmen in their duties of practice and wall patrols.

The restlessness he felt was not new. It returned whenever he remained at the keep as if his destiny was not there, but elsewhere. He considered that perhaps if the laird allowed him to be posted in Taernsby, he could work at the southern post while making a home there. Otherwise, he would have to leave his work as a guard.

The thought surprised him, but if he were to be honest, he wanted to be a leader. If not a leader then he would feel he'd let both the laird and himself down.

THE MORNING OF departure, Darach Ross stood before him and the ten archers who were to return with him.

"I do not wish for war with the villagers of Creag. There is a long-standing historical treaty between them and Clan Ross. However, I will not stand for any more attacks on our people. They must be brought to heel."

Erik frowned, unsure what they were to do exactly if the laird did not declare war.

The laird must have read his mind. "Erik, ye and the entire contingent are to go to the village and ensure the council understands we have every intention of remaining in place and anyone trespassing on our lands will be dealt with."

"Killed?" An archer behind him asked. "Can we shoot them down?"

Darach looked past Erik to the man, and he turned to see who it was. The lithe young man had an eager expression.

"If they are up in a tree armed with a bow and arrow, then aye, ye may."

The archers exchanged looks and nodded in agreement.

"Any other questions?" The laird scanned the faces and at the lack of responses, returned his attention to Erik. "What say ye?"

Turning to face the ten men, Erik spoke next. "There are guard quarters, each of ye should have enough room for a cot. The stables will have to be made larger. It will not take long. The travel there is easy, but the duties upon arrival are not."

SOON THEREAFTER, HE and the contingent of archers rode across the lands toward Welland. It meant he could not stop in Taernsby to see Esme, but Erik expected to be able to visit her in a few days.

The ride back was not as comfortable as his ride to the keep. They were met with a steady rain.

Finally two days after leaving Keep Ross, the sodden group arrived at the camp late in the day.

Torac and Struan met Erik waiting for him to fill them in on what occurred while the guardsmen were instructed to help the archers settle in.

The rain continued pelting the roof as he and the two men sat in the smaller building, which also housed Balgair and Graeme, but the two men had left to allow the leaders privacy.

"I like the idea of confronting them. Hopefully, it will bring this all to an end," Torac stated. "Ten archers, plus our men, will make a strong point."

Struan huffed. "I would prefer to attack. I do not believe discussion is what these people understand."

Erik had to agree with Struan. "What I do not understand is why we adhere to the treaty, but they do not."

The other two nodded in agreement. "Nevertheless, we must do what our laird directs. A show of force and shoot down idiots in trees," Torac said.

"There was an occurrence while ye were gone," Struan said. "The boy, Laith, he ran away."

Anger boiled at the boy's lack of patience. "Where did ye run to?"

"We think back to the village," Struan replied. "Probably worried about his sister."

"His sister is in Taernsby. I took her there myself."

The two men looked to him in expectation of what he'd say next. "She is the one who left the man, Tavon, for dead after he dragged her to the woods."

"Why did ye take her to Taernsby?" Struan asked. "Is the leader of the guard aware?"

"Aye, both Quinn and Gavin are aware. I didnae wish to leave her in the forest, was not sure what else to do with her."

Torac met his gaze. "Ye care about the lass. It could prove dangerous. I truly hope she is not lying to ye."

Despite understanding why Torac doubted Esme's intention, especially now with Laith going back to the village, it annoyed him.

"She is not lying. If ye would have seen the state of her, ye would understand. Either way, she will be watched there at the village."

"I suppose there isn't a way for her to report anything back from there," Torac replied.

THANKFULLY THE NEXT morning, the rain had subsided enough for them to restart the bonfire and gather outside.

The men ate a simple first meal of porridge, bread, and eggs, having to eat in shifts as there were too many for Auley and his helper to feed at once.

"We will have to hire help for Auley," Struan said between bites.

"And build more tables," Balgair added as he ate standing next to Erik and Struan.

Just then Torac called the men to listen and began giving instructions for the day.

"The new archers are to work on building cots for themselves." He motioned to a group of warriors. "See about extending the stables to ensure proper shelter for all the horses."

Erik went to where Torac stood. "The rest of ye will ride along the perimeter of our lands and ensure safe passage for any travelers. Be sure ye remain on the safe paths. Do not venture into the forest."

As the men divided and either went to chop down trees to build things or mounted to patrol the roads, Erik asked Struan to go with him to the village.

"I will remain and oversee things," Torac said. "I plan to patrol the shoreline with a couple of men."

BY THE END of the day, most of the work was completed and much to Auley's delight a family arrived to help with the kitchen duties. A man, wife, and daughter arrived by cart, along with a pair of dogs that happily raced to the men, tails wagging as if they were the reason for the gathering.

Struan looked on with a pained expression. "A family?" he asked Erik. "Why?"

"Before arriving at Welland, they cooked for a wealthy merchant in the north. The merchant died and they were left without work. They planned to settle here and have yet to find a home."

"The daughter is bonnie. Could be a problem," Struan retorted. "Too many men about."

"Perhaps ye can keep her safe?" Erik replied with a pointed look. "She is quite bonnie."

Struan huffed. "We have better things to do. That is her da's job."

It was easy to find volunteers to build a cottage for the family. Guardsmen tripped over themselves to catch a glimpse of the new cook's daughter. However, one stern look from her rather robust father kept them at bay.

"When do we go to Creag?" Torac asked, walking up to Erik that evening as he ate last meal. The new cook had helped Auley slaughter a boar and they'd roasted it. The meal was delicious.

"Perhaps the day after tomorrow. We must proceed in the best possible manner."

A man on horseback galloped toward the camp and instantly, everyone stood to see who it was.

"Quinn sent me to speak to Erik Larsen," the man called out.

Upon Erik standing, he spoke again. "We require yer assistance. The encroachers have returned. There are more this time. Perhaps fifty." The scout did not bother dismounting.

Names were called and ten men were to remain behind. Within minutes, a group of about thirty, including the healer, Graeme, was mounted and headed toward Taernsby. Erik prayed the attacks were not near the village and that Esme was unharmed.

IT WAS FAR worse than Erik expected, men fought on horseback and on foot. Several lay on the ground, either dead or badly injured. It was easy to tell who the Ross warriors were as they all wore the same style dress of well-made tunics and breeches, while the other men wore thick leather trews and fur-lined overcoats. They had to be from the upper isles.

The climate of the battle changed when he and his men entered the fray, and the encroachers took up defensive positions, fighting while retreating.

"There is nowhere for ye to go," Erik screamed at the man he fought against. "This isle belongs to Clan Ross."

The man thrust his sword forward and Erik jumped to keep from being cut. At the evasive maneuver the man sliced through the air again, the tip of his blade dangerously close. Thankfully Erik managed to block the strike while holding up his shield to defend himself from another aggressor.

Across from him, Erik noted that Graeme had dropped his healer's box and drawn a sword. The healer fought with grace and precision, easily besting his opponent.

The Ross men were outnumbered, but not by much. At several points, Erik found himself fighting two men using both his sword and shield to attack and protect at the same time.

He was growing tired, as it was hard to beat a pair of well-trained men. Turning to swing his sword, a hard hit to the back of his head made him see stars.

The next blow sent him falling to the ground. To keep from being slain, Erik rolled to his back and held up the shield. It was too hard to stand as he was surrounded by both sides.

Finally, he scrambled to his feet just in time to fight an aggressor who was caught by surprise, obviously expecting to kill him.

The fighting continued and free of his opponent, Erik raced to help Torac who fought against three and managed to down one of them.

The entire time the attackers called out commands, seeming well organized in battle, their tactics very different than the Ross warriors.

At the sound of a horn, the enemy fighters rushed forward in a synchronized pattern, their swords moving in a cross pattern.

Arrows flew through the air, impaling the enemy fighters. One by one they fell to the ground, caught by surprise at the arrival of a long line of archers on horseback.

"Where the hell have they been?" Balgair called out.

"They could not shoot arrows as we fought. Much too dangerous," Torac called out.

Seeming to realize the battle was lost, the attackers dropped their swords and surrendered.

Erik and Torac hurried to the injured to see who required immediate help. Thankfully, there were two healers, the one from the southern post arrived just as Graeme began working.

Four of his men were injured and two were dead. More dead. Erik kneeled next to one of the fallen, the man had been cut across the neck.

He placed a hand on the warrior's shoulder and leaned

over him. "Rest now brave one." He then went to the other who'd been cut through. The dead man's eyes stared blankly at the sky.

Erik repeated the words to this man and let out a long breath. This warrior had a wife and bairns. The woman would be heartbroken.

With an angry growl, he hurried to where the prisoners were. The men were tied, ankles and wrists bound. There were about twenty of them.

"I counted the injured and dead. Some must have escaped," Gavin gritted out the words. He called out to his men, sending a group to search for those who'd gotten away.

"The bastards will not go far without horses."

"What do ye want?" Erik asked the closest bound man. "Why are ye here?"

The man spit at him, and Erik punched him, knocking him to the ground.

"They will talk," Torac said nearing. "It is a matter of time."

"I will help find those who escaped." Erik hurried to his horse. At feeling something trickling down his back, he reached to touch it. His fingertips were stained with his blood. Stumbling he reached for his horse, but all he felt was air. It was the same place where he'd been pierced before.

"Ye have been cut badly," a gruff voice said as Erik could no longer stand and crumpled to the ground.

CHAPTER THIRTEEN

A T THE SOUNDS of people calling out in urgent tones, Esme rushed to the window, threw open the shutters, and looked out.

There was a line of wagons leaving the village at a fast pace, while men on horseback rushed into the center of town, dismounted, and hurried into the constable's house.

Unsure of what happened, she grabbed her shawl and ran down the stairs to where Flora stood by the door.

"What happens?" Esme asked watching as men rushed out from the constable's house to the town square.

The constable began calling for people to come out and she along with Flora hurried to hear what was said.

"There was a battle on the hills just outside the village. The injured will be brought here. We need beds for those who need care."

Flora lifted her hand. "I can keep two in my house. I will clear out the front room."

The constable acknowledged her, and they listened as more volunteered either space or help. Finally, she and Flora headed back to Flora's house and began making room for whoever would be cared for.

"Does this happen often?" Esme asked as she dragged a chair over to where Flora instructed. She seemed to have things well in hand knowing what to put where.

"This village has dealt with many things over the years. When I was rescued from the sea and treated so well after coming ashore. I vowed to do what I can to help in times such as these. 'Tis the way of life, I suppose."

Flora waved people in who came carrying items needed to set up the cots. In a matter of minutes, two comfortable—but firm—beds, along with side tables and chairs transformed what had been a sitting room into a satisfactory place for the injured.

They went to wait and as they did, the warrior Gavin came to them. He was dirty and blood was splattered across his tunic.

"Are ye harmed?" Flora asked studying him.

The warrior shook his head. "Nay. I was told ye have two beds?" He met Esme's gaze for a short moment. "Erik is one of the injured. I will have him brought here."

At the mention of Erik's name, Esme's breath caught. "Is it serious?"

"I do not know." The warrior called out to a man driving a wagon. "Bring them here."

The first injured man groaned loudly when moved. It was obvious he was in a great deal of pain. His face was covered in dirt and blood, so it was hard to tell what he looked like. Flora directed the men who carried him to where he could be settled.

Unlike the first man, Erik was silent. Eyes closed. Head to the side. He seemed to be asleep. Esme motioned to the empty cot. "Here. Place him here." She looked past them.

"Where is the healer?"

"Still at the battlefield," one of the men replied. "Some of the injured cannot be moved."

Once the injured men were settled, Flora became animated. "Bring the pot of boiling water from the hearth," she directed. Then to Esme's astonishment, she brought out a basket full of strips of cloth and a wooden box with amber bottles filled with liquids and herbs and headed over to Erik.

She met Esme's gaze. "It is not always the one who is making all the noise who is injured worse." Her eyes slid to the man who continued to groan, then looked to Erik.

"First we must remove their clothing and inspect their bodies for injuries."

With the help of the men who'd carried them in, they undressed them both. Flora looked the groaning man over and they found he'd been cut through on his left side under his arm and his right arm was broken.

Erik bled from a cut to his head and from his lower back. Flora poured water to clear the blood from the head wound. "Quite deep," she said. "There is not much to be done, but to wrap it and wait for him to wake."

The cut to his back was not too big or deep, for which Esme was glad. Flora instructed Esme to wash it out and sew it shut.

As she worked, Esme was glad he was unconscious as it would have been terribly painful. A warrior stood by to assist in case Erik came to. She noted the man winced a couple times as the needle broke through the flesh.

"It will leave a scar," Esme said trying to cut the tension. The man nodded. "'Tis not his first in the same place."

Once she finished, they rolled him onto his back. A blanket

was thrown across his midsection for modesty, leaving the rest of Erik's body on full display. Despite his state, it was hard not to admire his well-muscled build. He was perfect to her, despite old scars that crossed his abdomen, upper chest, and left shoulder. She'd not seen them when they'd been together as there'd not been much light.

It was a wonder how much warriors suffered in their duties to defend the clan.

Once she finished washing Erik, they changed the blankets, and he was covered with a clean blanket and left to rest.

The other warrior turned out the be Quinn, who she'd met before. He was not as easy to work with. Cleaning and sewing his wounds meant moving him, which caused a great deal of pain. By the time they finished with him, both he and everyone else were exhausted.

Flora gave him a mixture of herbs to drink, and he lay still waiting for the effects, but from his pinched expression, he obviously continued to be in pain.

"Would ye like something else to drink or eat?" Esme asked the injured man.

He shook his head and stared up at the ceiling.

Sitting next to Erik, she touched his arm, rubbing her hand up and down the warm skin. "Erik, can ye hear me?"

He didn't react. It was only the steady lifting and lowering of his chest that gave her comfort.

"Can ye go to the market and get food?" Flora asked from the door that led to the kitchen. "Carrots, leeks, perhaps bread."

Esme stood and looked down at her bloody dress. "I will change and go see about it. With all that's happened, I forgot about eating."

More than anything, she wanted to know who they'd fought and whether her village was involved. However, she didn't dare ask anyone but Erik, and he was still unconscious.

The market was abuzz, mostly people standing in circles discussing the battle and who was there to be cared for.

Apparently, not all the injured brought to be cared for were Clan Ross. Several men who fought against them were housed nearby. It seemed the kind people of the village had taken it upon themselves to go and fetch a pair of men who'd been left behind on the field by Ross warriors still alive.

She walked to a circle of women who spoke with animation. Upon noticing her, they asked about who she and Flora were caring for.

"Ah, the lovely Quinn," one said. "How does he fare?"

Esme wondered why they considered Quinn to be lovely. The man—although ruggedly handsome—seemed quite gruff. "He has a broken arm and several other injuries, but he will recover."

"Who is the other?" a young woman asked. "I hear he is the blond Viking."

"Aye," Esme replied and studied the woman who seemed very interested. "He has not come awake as of yet."

"Oh, dear," the same woman said. "I will go and help Flora." She hurried away in the direction of Flora's house.

At the vegetable stand, she purchased what was needed and then hurried to the bakery where the aroma of the baking bread made her mouth water. Instead of one loaf, she bought two.

Guards stood outside the doorway, and she hesitated at

recognizing them. They were Erik's men. Too engrossed in the conversation, they did not pay her any heed.

"The boy ran away, then the attack happens. I do not trust it. He is probably a spy."

"Aye, used by the council no doubt."

"These men were not part of the village, they may have nothing to do with it."

"Nonetheless, why did the boy leave? Erik can be too trusting. Neither he nor his sister should be near our camp."

She'd moved to stand beside the building, so they did not notice her as she covered her mouth. Had Laith returned to the village? Was it to look for her?

When the men changed the subject and walked away, she hurried back to Flora's more desperate than ever for Erik to awaken.

To her relief, Erik was indeed awake and upon seeing her tried to sit up, only to fall back on the bed and hold his hands up to cradle his head. "That hurt," he murmured.

"I am glad to see that ye are awake," Esme said wondering how soon she could ask him what happened.

Flora walked in. "Aye, he awoke just as ye left." She glanced at the basket. "Would ye mind cooking?"

"Of course not." Esme glanced at Erik who squeezed his eyes shut from the pain in his head.

They helped the two injured men eat, with the help of the woman who'd rushed over earlier and had not left Erik's side since. Esme was too exhausted to care about the woman's flirtations at the moment, what she wanted was to ask about her brother.

Unable to speak to Erik, who promptly fell asleep after

eating, Esme went to her room to rest.

When she woke it was late in the day. She hurried to Flora's house. Upon walking in, she was surprised to see Erik standing and dressed. He spoke to Quinn in quiet tones.

"What can I do to help right now?" Esme asked Flora.

"I will be here a bit longer although Quinn is well enough to be left alone," Flora replied. "Come in the morning."

"Very well," she looked to Erik. "Are ye leaving now?"

"I will walk with ye," he said, and they went out to the chilled night.

"I must speak to ye," Esme stated in a hushed tone. "Do ye wish to come to my...?"

"Nay, I cannot," he interrupted. "I must go to see about my men and then ride to the guard post here."

Of course, it was understandable. He had duties that were more important at the moment. However, it was as if he kept her at a distance, not even bothering to thank her for what she'd done.

"What do ye wish to speak to me about?" There was a warmth in his gaze, although perhaps it was just wishful thinking on her part. "Is something wrong?"

"My brother. I overheard that he'd gone. Do ye know where he went?"

Erik let out a breath, by the tightness between his brows, his head still ached. "Esme, at the moment I have more important matters to see to than yer brother acting like a child and running off in the night without a word of appreciation for what my men did for him."

"I must go see about my injured men," he said stopping at the seamstress shop. He touched her upper arm. "We can speak later." With that, he left.

THE NEXT MORNING, Esme was more distraught than ever. What if Laith was being held and mistreated by the council because of what happened to Tavon?

It was probable they knew she was to blame for his injuries. If Tavon was still alive and regained consciousness, he would name her as trying to kill him.

If only Laith had stayed at the Ross camp and waited. He must have heard about what happened or was worried about her and had decided to return for her.

Tears slipped down her face as she wondered what was best to do. There were so many obstacles in the way of her going for her brother. But if he had been caught, they would punish Laith expecting that he knew where she was. There was no choice, she had to go to Creag and find Laith.

In a large basket, Esme placed several pieces of clothing she rolled tightly. Next she placed a cloth over it, to make it seem as if she carried a meal. She walked from the seamstress shop to the village square. All seemed to have returned to normal. When she neared a stand where a husband and wife sold roasted meat atop bread, she purchased one, wrapped it in a cloth, and placed it in her basket.

"Is there any news of any ongoing threat?" she asked the woman who shook her head.

"We heard a ship was spotted leaving. It was hidden by the thick forest and hills." The woman motioned to the side away from the village.

"That is good news, I suppose," Esme said with relief at the knowledge that any threat against Erik and his men was gone.

After that, she walked across and slipped between the baker's shop and a home, from there it was open land. Deciding it was best to walk closer to the shore and make her way back to her village that way, she began what would be at least two days of walking.

It was late in the day when Esme finally found a tiny, abandoned cottage with half the roof missing. The walls would protect her from the wind and if she slept under the covered portion, it would be somewhat dry.

Thankfully it had not rained that day. Other than a light mist in the morning, the rest of the day remained cloudy, but dry.

Once inside the structure, she used branches and twigs to block any night foraging beast from entering the open doorway. Once that was complete, she lowered to the floor using the thick cloak Erik had bought for her to keep warm.

The sounds of the night lulled her mind and her body to relax as she ate the food she'd purchased. Hopefully by the end of the next day, she would find Laith.

CHAPTER FOURTEEN

T HE SUNSHINE STREAMING through the window made Lattie sit straight up. It had to be late morning, and yet the house was quiet.

She hurriedly rose from the bed and yawned widely. It had been a sleepless night. Her youngest cried nonstop, the teething ruining not only his night but hers as well.

Ian had gotten up and gone to sleep in the other children's room. He'd probably gotten more rest there.

Rushing down the stairs, she walked into the kitchen to find her mother-in-law in the doorway peering out to the garden with the youngest in her arms. Swaying side to side, she spoke in low tones to the cooing bairn.

"Ye are magical, I don't know how ye keep him so quiet," Lattie said in a low voice. "Where are the others?" she said referring to her three other sons.

"Planting," her mother-in-law replied motioning to the door with her head.

Indeed outside, the three lads were digging holes and carefully placing seeds into each one. Then they covered them up and stepped on the dirt to ensure it was firm.

"How?" Lattie asked then gawked back at the boys. "They grumble when I ask them."

Her mother-in-law smiled. "They had a choice, either

plant or scrub the floors. Whichever their choice was, they were to remain quiet and allow ye to sleep. I promised a tart later."

Lattie lowered to a chair. "And Ian?"

"He went to the market. Asked that ye come when ye are ready. Not to hurry."

The thought of her gruff husband selling vegetables made her smile. "I am so very blessed to have ye and him in my life."

When Ian's mother moved in, it had been an adjustment as the woman criticized everything Lattie did. However, over the last few months, through all the distress of the council becoming more oppressive, they'd become closer.

She had pulled Lattie aside one morning and said, "If we are to survive this, we must be stronger as a family." After that, they'd gotten along much better.

WITH HER TWO eldest boys in tow, Lattie headed to the market to relieve Ian from selling at the square. Her mother-in-law insisted on keeping the two younger boys, for which Lattie was grateful.

"What happens?" her eldest asked pointing to a group of people who'd gathered.

"I do not know." Lattie held the boys back and watched as the group parted for Colin, the tavern owner, who carried a boy toward his home.

Lattie hurried over trying to see who the injured person was, but it was hard to tell.

"What happened?" she asked Ian, whose face looked as if carved from stone.

"Probably Fergus and the like. Beat the poor lad unconscious."

"Why would they do that?" Lattie asked. "He is but a lad."

Ian seemed to have not heard her. She'd never seen her usually passive husband so angry. "We cannot continue to stand by as they do whatever they want to us?"

A man neared; his arms crossed over his large chest. "I agree. Something must be done."

"What happens next?" Ian asked emboldened by the man's presence. "How long will we stand by?"

Lattie stared up at her normally quiet husband. "I am scared. Going against the council can bring danger to our bairns."

"Come here." She motioned for the boys who'd run after Colin. "Now!"

The lads came back to her, eyes wide. "It is Laith. He looks almost dead."

"Why is he here?" Lattie whispered to Ian. "Why did he return from where he was?"

"My guess is he is searching for Esme."

Lattie hurried to see about the boy, her heart pounding so hard it threatened to explode from her chest. This was horrible. As of late, the way the council dealt with things was becoming worse.

Although she feared what was to come, Lattie had to agree with her husband. They had to do something, the mistreatment of the defenseless without consequence could not be allowed to continue.

"Lattie," Laith's voice was barely a whisper. "M-my sister?"

"She is gone from here," Lattie replied, not wishing to lie to the lad who began to cry when Colin's wife, Claire, started to clean his wounds. "What happened?"

"Th-they think I know where she is," Laith said before promptly passing out.

"'Tis good," the tavern owner's wife said. "He will not feel the pain of me having to sew shut the deeper cuts."

"What did they do?"

The woman gave her a knowing look. "Someone with a ring hit him about the face. My guess by the bruising is that they also punched and kicked him until he managed to run away. Poor thing."

Lattie helped clean the wounds, there was not much else that could be done for the other injuries. They wrapped his chest tight in case his ribs were broken and then covered him up to allow him to rest.

When she returned to the stand, Ian was nowhere to be found, their eldest son stood by looking annoyed at missing whatever was happening.

Across the square a group of men, including her husband, were gathered.

Lattie let out a long sigh and peered up at the cloudy sky. Unless something happened soon, her village would be consumed with hate and war.

"WE MEET WITH the warriors from Taernsby here, at dawn." Erik stated pointing at an area on the rough map Torac had drawn. Surrounded by the warriors, the responsibility of not only his men's lives, but also the clans' people's lives, was a heavy but welcome burden Erik shouldered with pride.

"As soon as the men from Taernsby arrive, we will ride from here," Torac pointed to an area just south of the camp where they could gather with the other warriors and head toward the village without being spotted until they were very close to the gates.

"We will ride in lines of four across," Eric said, looking up to meet Struan's gaze. "We must make a show of force and ensure they are aware Clan Ross is not to be toyed with."

Balgair growled out a sound of approval. "About time."

"A rider approaches," someone called out as a man rode closer. "I seek Erik!" he called out.

Erik lifted a hand. "What happens?"

The man looked to the others seeming reluctant to speak. "Gavin asks that I speak to ye in private."

When Torac gave Erik a pointed look, he shook his head. "Tell me, what is it?"

"The woman. The one ye brought. She left Taernsby."

The air stilled. Every pair of eyes on him. "Gavin asks if we come in the morning or wait for ye to find her?"

By the tightening around Torac and Balgair's mouths, they were fighting to keep from cursing.

ESME WOKE WITH a start. She'd slept much too long, exhausted from the long walk and anxiousness.

She'd been lucky to make it to the village by nightfall. Annoyed, she got up from the nest she'd made with leaves and shook out the cloak. After removing the branches that had kept the doorway blocked, she walked out and turned in a circle.

"Oh, no," she said softly unsure which way to go. When she'd spotted the cottage through the trees, she kept winding her way through the forest until she reached it. She had been so exhausted she hadn't thought to take heed of which direction she had come.

After retracing her steps as best she could remember, Esme came to a path. But as time passed, the more certain she became she was utterly lost. Everything looked the same—unfamiliar and foreign.

The wind blew and she sniffed the salty air. Moments later through the foliage, she could see the shoreline. But to know which way to go, she had to leave the shelter of the trees. The laps of the waves against the shore promised a peace that did not exist. The lulling sounds welcoming a weary traveler to rest almost made her cry.

As she carefully made her way to the beach, she remained vigilant. Pausing to listen for anyone who might be about. But once there, she realized it was for nowt, as nothing told her which direction was which. Everything was the same. Every way she looked. Even the sky was of no use. Filled with clouds it did not allow her to see the position of the sun.

Esme threw her head back and let out a primal scream. It seemed no matter how hard she fought, obstacles blocked her at every turn.

How had she allowed herself to become so utterly lost?

There was only one thing to do, and it was to follow her instincts and keep moving. Whether in the right direction or the wrong one, as long as she put one foot in front of the other, it meant she did not give up.

She returned to the shelter of the trees and soon lost sight of the shore. Tears trailed down her face in annoyance.

It was hard to tell how much time had passed and still there was nothing familiar in the surroundings. When she came upon a berry bush, she stopped and plucked the fat sweet offerings. Eating only a few, not wishing to eat too many and become ill.

Suddenly she was grabbed around the waist and whirled around, Esme gasped in horror. Her entire body tightened, and she began kicking.

"Stop it at once." Erik's stern voice was like a slap of cold water and Esme shrunk back.

"How…how…" All she could do was stutter.

He took her by the upper arm. "Come." They walked in silence to where his steed waited.

"I have to go see about my brother," she said trying to explain.

When he looked at her, she saw not the man who'd been her gentle lover, but a warrior. There was a fierceness in his gaze that Esme had not seen before. "What ye will do is return to yer room in Taernsby and remain there until it is safe. My men and I are going to yer village. We were to go today, but this decision of yers to wander off means we must now go tomorrow."

"Ye did not have to—" Esme began, but he interrupted.

"Aye, ye are right. I did not, but I promised to look after ye."

She frowned and glared up at him. "I can take care of myself. I do not require ye to do so. Ye have things to do and so do I. I want to ensure my brother is not killed by those bastards that are allowed to do with us as they please. If ye do not understand that, then there is nothing else to be said between us."

Esme yanked her arm from his hand. "I will continue on my way."

"Ye were headed north. It is at least a day's ride back to Taernsby. By foot two days or more to yer village."

She allowed him to take her back to the horse. After lifting her to the saddle, he mounted and guided the horse into a gallop. Esme no longer cared where he took her. Once she rested, she would hire someone to take her to her village.

They rode in silence, Erik rigid in the seat. Once her mind settled, she realized he'd ridden quite a long way to find her despite his injury. To add that guilt to her burden would have made continuing impossible, so she pushed it from her mind.

The village appeared as they crested a hill and soon he deposited her in front of the seamstress shop.

Esme looked up at him. "Understand me. I must see about my brother."

It was evident from his taut expression, he was not interested in anything she had to say. "There is more going on right now than ye and yer brother. We are doing what we can to save lives. Ye are not helping."

Anger surged. "Do not blame me. Ye did not have to come after me. I will do what I must."

"Do as ye wish. It is obvious ye do not listen to me and do not require anything of me," Erik replied.

The words sunk into her chest making it hard to breathe and she realized how her own words earlier had made Erik feel. She closed her eyes.

"It is just that I am truly worried about Laith. Would ye not be in my place? Despite what he did."

Erik shook his head. "What do ye think to have accomplished by going there alone?"

"I cannot just sit here and do nothing."

"I ask that ye stay here. If ye do not heed what I say, there is little I can do."

More than anything she wanted him to show even a small bit of care, to try to understand how she felt, but it was as if he could not move past being angry with her.

"Fine." Esme pushed past him and hurried up to her room above the seamstresses' shop.

Inside her room everything was just as she'd left it. Taking a seat at the table by the wall, Esme considered what she should do. What would be for the best? Find someone to take her back? Or remain here and wait as Erik wanted?

Surely if Erik went to the village and found Laith, he would tell her where he was. Although he was angry—and had every right to be—he was not a cruel man.

As the day turned to night, Esme stared up at the stars and considered that somewhere, under the blanket of the night sky, there were people who were happy. Families who did not have the worries of surviving day to day. Somewhere under the blanket of lights, there was hope and there was love.

Perhaps one day she would be one of those people.

CHAPTER FIFTEEN

C LAN ROSS WARRIORS formed four lines of ten men. Along the front, Erik was joined by Torac, Struan, Balgair, Gavin, and Quinn, who'd traveled from Taernsby—despite his injuries—to assist.

They would make a formidable site upon arriving at Creag. Whether the council wished to cooperate or not, it was too late, they would not be given a choice.

Despite Darach wanting to keep the treaty in place, the men of Creag did not have to know Clan Ross would continue to honor it. However, the killing of their men was not something that would be forgiven. That was a debt they intended on repaying.

They arrived at the village just as the sun was setting.

A scout came toward them, the man so lithe the rider and horse seemed as one. "There seems to be a rebellion forming. A lad was left for dead with the council's blessing and the people of the village have finally had enough."

"That is good news," Torac replied. "It is about time the villagers realize they outnumber the idiots who consider themselves in charge."

"Let us go," Erik commanded, and they galloped to the village, raising their shields as they neared. There weren't any archers in the trees surrounding the entrance to Creag, which was strange. Perhaps the people who'd been defending the council were now part of the rebellion.

As they continued through the village toward the center of town at a rapid pace, people ran away. Though even as they hid in their cottages, they openly gawked out their windows with curiosity.

In the village square a large group of men along with a few women had gathered. They stopped speaking and turned to look at Erik and his men approached.

When they came to a stop a trio of men came to stand in front of the others.

"Where is the council?" Quinn called out.

"Hiding in there!" a young lad yelled pointing to a large house.

One of the three men met Erik's gaze. "They ordered the lad, Laith, to be beaten. It is time for us to see about replacing the council. We do not require yer help in this."

For a second, Erik winced at the information about Laith, but he pushed it aside. "We do not wish to involve ourselves in the issues of yer people. However, I have no doubt that some of ye standing here in this group have attacked some of our people."

There were murmurs and rumblings, the man who'd spoken turned to look over his shoulder and then looked back at them. "Aye, I am sure some have. In the future, it will be dealt with swiftly."

Torac and Struan dismounted and faced the trio. "Ye speak as if ye have already done away with the council, yet there they are—hiding."

The men exchanged looks and then looked to the cottage

where the council were supposedly hiding.

Erik spoke to Torac. "Let us go see about this." They continued forward with a few men, while the rest of the warriors formed a barrier around the structure to keep anyone from coming in or out.

Swords in hand, they rushed the front door and entered the dwelling to find a group of men, their wives, and several young who he assumed were their children.

"Come outside and face us," Erik called out. "Or we will burn this house to the ground with ye in it."

Slowly five men disengaged from crying women and pale younger children and walked out, each immediately flanked by Ross warriors.

The man called Rafe remained defiant. "We have a decades-old treaty with Clan Ross. Ye are not to interfere with our people…" He stopped talking when Balgair hit him so hard, he stumbled sideways with blood spurting from his nose.

"And ye were not to interfere with our people. Ye broke the treaty." Balgair spat at the ground and pushed the man to walk forward.

Villagers had gathered now, showing that they were quite a large population. That they'd allowed the five men before them to rule so harshly was annoying.

Erik walked to stand before the people. "We have no qualms with any of ye. Ye are and have always been free to travel to our lands without fear. Our people however have been constantly attacked and even killed by some of ye. Let today be a warning of what will occur if it happens again."

Torac stalked over to Rafe, who was cowering and trying to hide behind the older man next to him. Without hesitation,

Torac grabbed the man and sunk his broad sword into his chest. Loud gasps sounded as the villagers realized what happened.

Rafe's look of shock and disbelief as he collapsed told that he'd lived without fear of anyone ever questioning what he did.

"Ye cannot come and do this," a second councilman said. Erik knew he was who had directed that they beat Esme, so he motioned to Balgair. The warrior neared the man, who took a step backward, then without hesitation, cut his throat.

"Where is Tavon?" Erik called out.

One of the councilmen shook his head. "He is badly injured. Surely ye would not harm a sick man."

"Bring him." Erik did not care to hear any excuses. The man had mistreated Esme and he was sure she was not the only one.

There was a struggle as several villagers went into the dead councilman's house and dragged out a feverish-looking Tavon.

He looked to where his father lay dead and managed to escape the grips of those who held him. "Who did this?" he called out.

"Tavon!" The bearded burly man appeared. He narrowed his eyes at Erik but when spotting Balgair he growled and drew a large blade. "Get out of my village."

"They killed our Da, Fergus," Tavon said and walked forward. His gaze locked on Erik. "Ye did this, son of a whore."

"Nay," Erik said closing the distance. "But I did do this." He sliced across the man's throat. There was a look of shock on his face, followed by gurgling as blood spurted. Tavon gripped his hands around his throat, unable to keep the bleeding contained.

There was a united gasp from the gathered as Tavon fell to his knees and then face-first into the dirt.

"Bastard!" Fergus lifted his blade. Balgair crossed in front of the bearded man keeping him from nearing Erik and the two large men crossed swords. It was an unfair match as other than size, they were not equally matched in battle. Balgair quickly dispatched the man, who fell dead not far from his father and brother.

The remaining councilmen began begging for mercy.

"Ye may live," Erik said loudly, but ye must publicly renounce yer position as a council member and leave the village at once along with yer families."

With shaky voices, the three quickly agreed, while constantly looking over to the dead.

"Who takes responsibility for the village, so we know who to speak to in the future?" Erik called out.

The same trio came forward. One was called Ian. One was called Grant. And the one called Colin spoke to Erik. "The lad, he is in the tavern. He will survive."

It was obvious they were aware he knew Esme. Erik nodded and walked closer to the man. "Tell him his sister is well and in Taernsby."

TORAC AND STRUAN remained to speak to the new self-appointed council. Erik and some of the men returned to camp, while the rest of the warriors remained back to wait for their leaders.

When Erik arrived at the camp, Auley awaited them with a hearty stew and freshly baked bread. It was oddly comforting to sit with the warriors and eat. It wasn't that he'd missed the camp, but more the feeling of accomplishment while keeping to the laird's orders and not battling.

Once Torac returned, they would ride out in groups on patrol to ensure it was safe. When that was settled, he would meet with the Clan Ross villagers and assure them it was once again safe to travel through the forest.

"The lass did not return then?" Auley asked Erik when he headed to check on the injured men.

Esme had made it very clear she did not to need him, and he wasn't sure what to think.

"I do not know if she will return," he replied annoyed that the man would remind him of Esme. For a few hours, he'd managed to push her out of his mind. The fact her brother was injured, and she would have to be informed, was something he wasn't sure how to deal with yet. He should have asked Gavin to do it. The man probably would have.

"'Tis a shame," Auley said shaking his head as if Erik had purposefully ruined his day. "'Tis a shame," the man repeated and ambled away toward the kitchen.

Graeme stood over an injured man who recovered from arrows piercing through several places on his back. When the healer looked up, he frowned at seeing Erik. "Are there more injured?"

"Nay," Erik replied. He peered down at the man who flinched when Graeme tugged stitches out. "How do ye fare?"

"I will live," the man replied. "How did things go?"

Erik spent a few moments informing the injured men about the occurrences in the village. Most of them welcomed the news with grunts of approval.

A FEW HOURS later, Torac and the archers returned. Erik went to speak to Torac, who sat and ate alone.

"Are matters settled, in yer opinion?" Erik asked as Struan walked over and lowered to sit with them.

Torac shrugged. "I believe so. The men who will lead now are aware of our expectations if they wish the treaty to remain in place."

"I believe they had enough of the old council and things will change," Struan added.

"What about the lad, is he to recover?"

For a moment, Torac was silent, then he met Erik's gaze. "The lass arrived just as we were leaving. She hired someone to bring her. I believe her presence will help her brother recover."

Erik wanted to groan with annoyance. Esme would do what she pleased and there was nothing anyone could do to change that about her.

"I told her to remain in Taernsby. What if there had been a battle? That would have been one more thing to see about. She is without regard for anyone but herself.

"I do not believe that to be true," Torac replied. "She asked about ye, if ye were unharmed. When hearing about her brother, she raced to see about him." The warrior looked past Erik. "She has no one but him. It is understandable she would go to great lengths to find him."

If his own family were in such a dangerous place, he would have done the same. Find them by any means possible and ensure their safety. Perhaps he should have helped her instead of taking her back and chastising her.

As the day came to an end and assignments were given out to the warriors for the next few days, Erik considered that perhaps he should go to Esme and see about her and her brother.

They had both said hurtful things to each other at parting.

He loved her and wanted a future with her. There was the matter of ensuring the safety of the people, but as soon as he could, it was best to speak to her and clear things. Ensure Esme still felt the same about him.

CHAPTER SIXTEEN

T HE NEW COUNCIL voted to give Esme and Laith the cottage that had belonged to Rafe. The wife and daughter had left a few days after his death to go live with family on the Isle of Barra. It was just as well as the villagers made it clear they were no longer welcome. The rest of the council had packed up and left with their families in tow.

The first days after returning, the village had been a bustle of activity. People were eager to continue with their lives, not having to worry about the oppression the old council held over them.

The new council, which consisted of three well-regarded men, set about meeting with the people and setting new rules. The laws, along with the punishments should ye break them, were well explained. They were fair, and the villagers seemed pleased.

Thankfully there was a lush vegetable garden at the cottage, and the well was but a short distance away. Esme set about working on making baskets so that they could afford other necessities. Laith was still not well enough to work, and he now walked with a pronounced limp, which meant he would not be able to do physical work again.

Ever resourceful, he began working with one of the villagers to learn arrow making. As a fletcher, he could earn coin

HILDIE McQUEEN

and it would not be as taxing for him.

Everything was working out much better than Esme could have imagined. Not only had she and Laith been given the large cottage, but they were now the owners of a mare and wagon Rafe's family had left behind. This meant she could travel to and from Ross lands to sell her wares.

One early afternoon, Esme was working near the creek cutting the long reeds she would need to make her intricate baskets when she saw a man standing on the opposite side of the creek watching her.

At first she did not recognize the man, but shading her eyes from the sun she realized it was Erik. He stood still next to his horse as the creature nibbled on the green grasses of the bank.

Her heart skipped and she swallowed down the feelings that had been bubbling just beneath the surface since she last laid eyes on him.

When he lifted a hand in greeting, she did not return it. She would not forgive him too easily for being so unbending when she needed him the most. If Erik wish to speak to her, he had to come and do it.

Esme closed her eyes as the memories of being with him flooded her mind. The feeling of his body against hers, the sensations that he'd brought from her.

When she opened her eyes, Erik was gone. For a moment, she wondered if it had all been an illusion.

The following day, as she again searched for perfect reed thin branches to make her baskets, she caught a glimpse of Erik. This time he rode past with several men. They hesitated at seeing her and like the day before, he held up a hand in greeting.

Esme lifted her hand, but then returned to her work, not wishing to see what they did. It was obvious they patrolled the forest to ensure there was no danger for their people. He'd not come to see her. Did that mean he'd not meant it when asking her to wait for him?

Would he leave at the completion of these duties?

It would be for the best. The more time passed, the easier it would be for her to forget him and move on.

"Lass, it is good to see ye." Hamish walked toward her, his hounds at his heels. The dogs rushed to her, tails wagging.

She petted heads and greeted Hamish. He asked about Laith, and she informed him of his progress.

"My son has never married, ye know," Hamish informed her. "He is in need of a wife."

"Although I know he is a good man, I do not wish for a husband," Esme told the man with a smile.

Hamish lifted a brow, the old man chuckling. "What about bairns? Do ye not wish to be a mother?"

Esme had often wondered why she'd not come to be with child. She'd been with two men, albeit one not by choice. When taken by force by Tavon, she'd been thankful that nothing ever came from it.

"I suppose I have not thought about it much, Hamish. Perhaps my time has passed."

"Nonsense," the old man protested. "Ye are still quite young."

Thankfully when they walked near to where Hamish lived, the son was not about. Esme greeted the old man's wife and hurried home to prepare that evening's meal.

As she cooked, once again her thoughts went to what Hamish had asked her. With the way her life had been, the last thing she'd wanted was to bring a child into it.

Now that things were more settled and she could consider marriage, Esme found that she did not desire it. She'd allowed her imagination free rein when thinking there was a future with Erik. Not now.

There was no other man for her. Of that she was sure.

"Esme?" Lattie opened the front door and peered in. "Did ye forget to come to the square today?"

Staring at her friend blankly, Esme tried to remember why she was to be at the square. "For?"

Lattie chuckled. "Ye wished to meet with the other women to discuss traveling to Ross lands to sell yer baskets."

"Oh, goodness," Esme exclaimed. "I forgot. I cannot believe it. Do not know where my mind is of late."

"I would say with a handsome blond man." Lattie walked to a chair and sat. "I must admit to liking that ye live closer. I can send the bairns over here to bother ye and get a few moments of quiet."

"Of course ye can," Esme said with a smile. "I love yer lads."

"Until ye have one of yer own."

What was it with everyone that day? Why did they keep bringing up bairns? Esme let out a sigh. "I will always love yers."

Lattie scrutinized her. "Ye look different."

"Perhaps it is that for the last sennight, I have eaten well and had a comfortable bed."

"Something else." Her friend's gaze moved down her body.

"Have ye had yer womanly flows?"

Esme huffed. "I am not with child if that is what ye are asking. Aye, I..." Her breath caught and she scrambled to remember the last time she'd had her flows. It couldn't have been that long before.

"I do not remember. Ye have me fretting now." Esme sat down and began thinking about it. Was it before she'd been with Erik or after?

"I should be having them shortly. It has only been a fortnight or so since."

Lattie shrugged. "Then ye have nothing to worry about.

Just as Esme's breathing settled, Lattie asked. "What would ye do if they do not come?"

WHEN THE FIRST week passed, Esme still did not worry about the possibility of what Lattie had said, however as the second week came and went, she began to accept the fact that she was indeed with child.

She was carrying Erik's bairn and was at a loss as to whether to tell him or not.

That he'd not come to see about her was frustrating. The more time passed, the more she was convinced he'd forgotten about her. He did not deserve to know about the bairn. Now that she had a home and would be supporting herself, she could provide well for a child.

A tear trickled down her face and she brushed it away. If nothing else, now she would have a beautiful reminder of falling in love.

"YE SHOULD TELL him," Lattie insisted for what seemed the hundredth time as they rode to Welland. Laith guided the mare, while Esme and Lattie sat in the back of the wagon with the collection of baskets and clay pots they planned to sell.

Esme looked to Laith, glad he didn't seem to be paying them any mind. Her brother was excited about selling the many arrows he'd made. Already he was gaining a reputation for making arrows that flew straight.

"I cannot tell him," Esme whispered. "It is best he does not feel obligated to me. Imagine life with someone who feels compelled by a sense of duty to be with ye while wishing for a different life. Both of us would be miserable."

Lattie rolled her eyes. "What both of ye are, is daft. It is obvious ye are enamored of one another."

"Shh," Esme said looking to Laith, who turned to look at them.

"Who is enamored?"

"Esme and the Ross guard," Lattie replied quickly. "Do ye not agree?"

Laith shrugged. "I thought so. But he hasn't come around."

AS THEY ARRIVED at the village, they were welcomed at the village square. The people were warm and excited to see the wares they had brought.

While she was glad at the welcome reception and the purchases, Esme kept an eye out for Ross guards who regularly patrolled. She didn't trust Lattie not to speak to Erik if the situation presented itself. Her friend was adamant that Erik had a right to know he'd sired a child.

Esme was too confused about it all to know what was best.

If only she had a mother, or if Mege was still alive. Someone experienced that would tell her what was best to do. For now, she went with her instinct and kept silent.

Just the thought of Erik rebuffing her and the bairn would be more than she could withstand. It would not be good for her or the child she carried to be rejected and heartbroken.

Although she'd lost so much in her life, there were still people she cared for and who cared for her. Colin and his wife, Hamish and his wife, and also Lattie and her family. She and Laith were finally safe and could concentrate on the days ahead without fear of being attacked.

Soon she would have to tell Laith about the bairn and she would need to tell him the truth. There would be no lies between her and her brother.

Esme studied her brother who was surrounded by men looking to purchase the arrows. Just in the weeks since going to the camp and returning, he'd become taller.

She felt as if Laith resembled their father, who she imagined had been tall and slender of build.

Neither she nor Laith remembered what their parents looked like. Every once in a while Esme would dream of a couple, but she could not see their faces. Time had erased them.

"Esme," Lattie said interrupting her thoughts. "Ye are almost sold out. It will be a quick trip today. I am going to purchase meat pies for our travel."

Her mouth watered at the thought. "I may eat mine before we leave."

"Ay, yer appetite has increased. It is something ye will have to pay heed to. Yer eating for two now."

Her gaze on Lattie's retreating figure, Esme sold the last two of her baskets.

A young woman neared and sighed in disappointment. "I hoped to catch ye before ye sold out. One of my neighbors purchased one of yer creations and I came as fast as I could. But I live at the farming community and could not arrive any sooner." The woman looked down, her face flushing just from speaking. It was obvious she was painfully shy.

"Where is the farm?" Esme asked.

"Not too far, in that direction, just past the grouping of trees," the young woman replied. She was pretty, with bright blue eyes and reddish-brown hair. "I am Leana, she said with a shy smile. Can I ask that ye save me one of yer beautiful baskets next time?"

Esme studied her for a moment. "Are there many families where ye live? Perhaps we can come there instead next time."

The young woman nodded. "Aye, about ten families."

"Very well. I will visit there as soon as I have enough made," Esme assured the young woman, who thanked her and then walked away.

AT THE SIGHT of a group of archers riding toward the village, her stomach dropped. They had to be Clan Ross warriors, and it was entirely possible Erik was with them.

The warriors rode to the tavern, near where Lattie had gone. Just then a man, who she recognized as the village constable, walked out and one of the warriors dismounted. They spoke for a few moments then the warrior remounted, and the contingent continued on through the village.

When Lattie returned, she handed Esme a meat pie and sat

next to her in the back of the wagon. "They are leaving. The archer told the constable, that most of the warriors were ordered to return to Keep Ross."

"It is understandable," Esme replied between bites of the deliciously cooked pie. The meat and potatoes in it were combined with a delicious thick sauce tucked inside flaky bread that had been baked perfectly.

"Aye, which is why ye should make haste and speak to Erik. What if he is also leaving?"

"It matters not," Esme insisted. "I have decided. I will not tell him, and I will not explain myself to the villagers either. Every one of them stood by while Tavon mistreated me without doing a thing to help. No one deserves to know who the father of my bairn is."

"Do ye not think the father has a right to know?" Lattie insisted.

Esme could not believe Lattie kept defending Erik. "Have ye seen him even once come see about me?"

At Lattie's lack of response, she continued.

"We both said things that perhaps we shouldn't have. But if his feelings were as strong as he professed, wouldn't he have at least tried to see me?"

"Men think very differently than us." Lattie began eating. "We should head back."

Esme let out a sigh.

As they ate, Laith walked back to the wagon, a wide smile on his face. He'd sold all of his arrows.

"Everything is going to be well," Esme whispered to herself.

CHAPTER SEVENTEEN

E RIK WALKED OUT into a bright morning. The sun burned the last of the haze away in the forest making it a magical sight. He stretched and walked to where Torac and Struan sat at a table eating.

Too much time had passed as they'd ensured all was well. He'd been called back to Keep Ross and returned. The patrols had proved that all was well and the news of a new council in Creag had spread.

"I am going to the village today," he said without preamble. "I am going to speak to Esme."

Neither man said anything.

For some reason he felt the need to explain. "I have a strong urge to see about her."

Struan chuckled. "Ye mean between yer legs?"

"Nay, in my gut. I cannot explain it."

The men exchanged looks, then cleared their throats. Obviously what he said made them uncomfortable. It was not the way of warriors to speak about feelings.

Finally, Torac cleared his throat. "Ye are fond of the lass. If ye decide to be with her, will ye leave service to the laird?"

It was a conversation he did not expect to have that morning upon waking. He'd caught glimpses of Esme over the last weeks. She looked well and without care. Each time, he'd been unable to approach her as he'd been patrolling and with other men.

But the night before, he'd dreamt of her. They'd been in the field between the forest and her village, and they'd embraced. It had felt so real, he'd woken expecting to see her in his bed.

"I am not considering anything more than speaking to her."

"We are to be left with a small contingent of warriors," Struan began. "Graeme has asked to remain. It seems there is no healer in Welland and the need for his talents is great."

Erik nodded. "If the laird approves."

Just then one of their warriors arrived and dismounted. "The laird arrives."

THEY SPENT THE rest of the day with Darach Ross, who wanted to visit the villages and meet the local people. Much to the delight of the people, who'd not been visited by the Ross in many years. There were nightly feasts, music, and revelry at both villages for several days.

By the fourth morning of his visit, Erik had given up on the idea of going to see Esme. He couldn't leave the camp while the laird was there. The man would give appointments for the next season, and he wished to be present when it occurred.

The laird looked to Erik. "I wish to visit the village that has caused so much trouble."

THE NEXT DAY, along with the laird's contingent of five warriors and five archers, Erik and Torac accompanied him to the village.

"It is larger than I remembered," Darach stated scanning the wide span of cottages, shops, and fields. "How many people live here?"

"Several hundred," Erik replied. "They are a sturdy lot. Not very friendly, but they have been under a very oppressive leader."

"Aye, I can understand then why they would not be a cheerful lot," Darach stated.

As expected the Ross was greeted, perhaps—not warmly—but the people seemed pleased that he'd come to visit.

The entire time they rode past cottages, Erik kept an eye out for either Laith or Esme. But he'd not spotted anyone familiar.

In the village square, the remnants of the fruit and vegetable stands remained, but most of the sellers had gone home.

Along with the laird, Erik walked into the tavern to meet with the new council. The men explained they wished to have a cordial relationship with Clan Ross, but they expected to remain independent of them.

As the conversation continued between Darach and the council, Erik walked outside and scanned the surrounding buildings. Laith sat outside a house working on something. Next to him was a tall basket filled with arrows. Erik recognized Esme's handiwork, the basket was well made. Head bent while working, he didn't notice Erik until he was close.

"I am glad to see ye," the young man said. "I wish to apologize for leaving without saying that I appreciate what ye did for my sister and me."

Erik reached for an arrow. "These are very well made. Do

ye sell them?"

"Aye, I do. Here and in Welland."

"I would like to purchase some." Erik silently chose some while Laith looked on.

The young man stood. "Wait, I have something for ye." He dashed into the house and returned with three arrows. "For ye. To thank ye for what ye did for Esme."

The workmanship was beautiful. The ends contained brightly colored feathers. "They are almost too nice to use," Erik said accepting them. "How is yer sister?"

Laith met his gaze. "She is not feeling well at the moment. But for the most part, we are doing better than we ever have."

"What do ye mean she doesn't feel well?"

"I should not have said anything," Laith replied rapidly. "Just a bit of an upset stomach."

"How long has she felt this way?" Erik looked past Laith to the doorway.

Laith shrugged. "Just a pair of days."

Everyone walked out of the tavern then, so Erik could not continue speaking to Laith. He handed the young man several coins that he reluctantly accepted and returned to where the men were now mounting.

"Did ye see her?" Torac asked.

Erik shook his head. "Was there anything of note said?"

"The laird promised safe passage to their people through-out our lands, he reminded them that any attack on our people would not be tolerated. Also that a contingent of Ross warriors would be remaining permanently where we currently are."

He'd expected as much. There were posts at every corner of Ross lands to protect both the people and their territory.

"I expect he will be speaking to us about who will be remaining here and for how long." Erik looked over his shoulder toward the village square. Laith continued to sit at the doorway working. He looked up and held up a hand in acknowledgment and Erik returned the gesture.

Over last meal, the laird praised all the men for the accomplishment both with the nearby village and assisting the warriors from the post at Taernsby.

He looked to Erik. "I wish ye to remain here permanently. Is there a problem with it?"

Erik shook his head. "No, Laird. I can remain."

As the laird asked each warrior, it was decided that fifteen warriors and the healer would remain. The warriors would be able to rotate between posts and back at the keep. The assignments and rotations were dictated by both the laird and his half-brother, Caelan Ross.

At dawn the next day, the laird, his contingent of warriors, and the warriors that were to return to the keep, left.

"It seems quiet," Torac stated as he and half of the men who remained prepared to go on patrol. "Are ye going to patrol today?"

"I have something to do."

When asked, Graeme agreed to travel with him to see about Esme. The two of them rode to the village and dismounted in front of Esme and Laith's home.

He hoped that the healer did not notice that his hand shook when he raised it to knock on the door.

CHAPTER EIGHTEEN

E SME'S FIRST THOUGHT upon rising that morning was to eat something. After days of retching and the inability to keep food down, it was not surprising that she was hungry.

After a full meal of toasted bread, porridge, and eggs, she pushed away from the table and headed to the back of the house to feed the chickens. Laith was gone with several others to sell their wares and she was glad for the peace. An entire day alone. However, at the same time, she would have to keep busy and not allow her mind to wander over what was to come.

Soon she would show, and people would begin to notice she was with child. There was nothing to be done about it and she would have to face the judgments that would surely come.

With a long sigh, she began sweeping out the chicken's pen when there were calls from the front of the house. Esme leaned her broom against the back door and walked through to the front. Upon opening it, her heart stopped.

Erik stood with a man she'd never met.

"Laith told me ye were ill. I brought the healer. Graeme. To see about ye."

"It was nothing. I feel much better." Esme directed her reply to the healer, who studied her with interest. "Upset stomach most mornings. Laith should not have mentioned it. It only happened a few times in the morning before I ate."

"He said it continued for days," Erik insisted. "Ye look a bit pale."

"It is because I have been indoors. Just now I was out back feeding my chickens because I am much better."

The healer continued to study her for a long moment. It was as if the man could see things others did not. Esme looked away from him and finally met Erik's gaze. "Ye should go."

"I will return to the camp then," the healer said once again studying her for a moment. "Ye should sit out in the sun and make oat cakes to settle yer stomach."

Esme felt the blood drain from her face. Did the man actually know she was with child just from studying her? The man walked away leaving her and Erik alone.

When Erik showed no sign of leaving, she gave him a questioning look. "I do not believe there is anything to be said between us."

Despite the lack of expression, his eyes darkened at meeting hers. It was as if he had so much to say but held it back. It took great effort for Esme to drag her gaze away. "Please go."

Glancing past her to the interior of the home, he once again looked at her. A smile played at the corners of his lips. Instantly Esme recalled what it was like to have his mouth on hers, to feel his lips on her body. She let out a shaky breath.

"I am glad to see that ye have a nice place to live. Both ye and Laith. If there is ever anything ye need. I am to remain at the camp permanently. Send word. I will be here."

Esme hitched her chin. "Why would I need help from ye? Laith and I can take care of each other. We always have."

"Ye do not have to depend only on him. There is nowt wrong with asking for help."

Heat rose up her body, even her face felt hot. Despite this, she maintained a level tone. "I have yet to see a reason to trust anyone. Everyone, Erik. Everyone leaves. It is best not to tie any hopes and dreams to another person. One day, I expect Laith will marry and leave as well. 'Tis the way of things."

His blue gaze met hers. He seemed at a loss for words. Finally, he lowered his eyes. "It has been yer experience. It is not always that way."

Once again she lifted her gaze to meet his. As much as she wished to ask him to stay, she knew it would only end up in heartbreak when he left her to return to his own life.

"Be with care." Erik turned away.

Unable to move, Esme remained in the doorway her gaze locked on his retreating form. Every fiber of her being taut with the desire to go after him, to touch him, and to be held in his embrace once again. Pride however kept her in place, her expression passive despite the slicing pain in her chest.

Her stomach revolted at all the food she'd eaten, and she rushed to the back of the house.

As if in revenge for turning the healer away, Esme was sick the rest of the day. Finally, she went to the doorway and called for a lad to go and fetch Lattie.

HER FRIEND TOOK one look at her as she sat in the back doorway, leaning on the frame with a bucket in front of her and hugged her.

"Sometimes while with child this occurs. I assure ye, it is nothing to worry about. But it is horrible to go through it."

"How long will I feel this way? I've felt well until the last few days. Are ye sure there is nothing wrong?"

Hot tears trailed down her face at feeling unable to do more than sit and pray for the nausea to relent. "I cannot see how I can go on like this. I have not been able to eat and keep food down for days."

"I will return shortly," Lattie said patting her shoulder. "Do not move. Seems ye are settling a bit."

Moments later, Lattie returned with a wooden bowl with dry flat oat cakes. "Try to eat these. Do not drink water. The dryness of the cakes will help ye feel better."

After three of the crisp cakes, Esme did indeed feel better.

"This is what the healer that came with Erik said I should eat."

"Erik was here?" Lattie's eyes went wide. "So he knows? And he left?"

Esme shook her head. "Nay, he does not know. I wonder if the healer suspects and will tell him."

"Did the healer treat ye?"

"I sent them away," Esme said. "It is probably a mistake. The bairn deserves to have a father."

Lattie gave her a droll look. "Talk to him."

ON THE RIDE back from Esme's village, Erik and Graeme came across a group of children playing. A dog joined in the fray much to the young ones' delight. They raced to the edge of the creek and began playing in the water.

"It is nice that they do not fear us," Graeme stated. "I often wonder why as humans mature, they become angry and do such horrible things, when as children all is fun and laughter."

Erik turned to the man. "Ye like children." It was obvious the healer took more than a passing interest in the young ones who played.

"Aye, I do. I have six nieces and four nephews; I enjoy visiting them."

"How many siblings do ye have?" Erik asked astonished.

Graeme laughed. "Two sisters who each have two. My three brothers each have one—so far."

They rode in silence as they crossed the creek where they knew the water was shallow. Graeme looked to him. "Is the lass important to ye?"

He decided to be honest. "Aye, she is. I thought to settle with her. But now I am not sure how she feels about me. She will not speak to me. In truth, I am confused about how I feel."

The healer let out a breath. "I suspect the reason of her ailment is that she may be with child."

Graeme's words seemed to float in the air, each one sinking slowly into his mind. For a moment he forgot how to breathe until his lungs protested and he took in a big gulp of air.

"With... child?"

The healer shrugged. "I could be wrong. She complained of feeling badly in the mornings. That is usually what happens during the first months."

Words did not form. Looking over his shoulder, he considered going back immediately.

"We had a disagreement, said things we should not have. I have been away... with duties. I find that I am brave in battle, but a bit of a coward when stating my feelings."

Graeme nodded. "'Tis how it is when our emotions take

over."

Mind reeling, he did not ride back to the camp with Graeme but made the excuse of going to Welland and rode straight to the eastern shoreline.

The salty air soothed his mind instantly. The sounds of the sea and the swells of the waves were inviting. He dismounted and sat on a fallen tree that had been dragged there by the locals to use for this exact purpose.

Birds dashed along the water's edge searching for bits to eat in a playful display. But no matter how calming the sea was, he could not keep his thoughts from returning to Esme and how he would approach her.

Since leaving her at Taernsby, she was the first thing he thought about each day. Often he'd considered how he missed her smile. The way she'd looked at him after they'd made love the first time. There had been pure trust and innocence in her eyes. Now that was gone.

He'd been too hard on her when she'd gone to search for her brother. Acted as if he didn't care. In truth, he'd been terrified that she had been hurt or worse. That the men from Creag had found her and made her pay for Tavon's death.

Instead of understanding her, he'd been rigid, not comforting her or offering to help. She'd asked him what he would have done in her place, and he'd not replied. Of course he would have done the same. Gone after his siblings to ensure they were unharmed.

He loved her. It was plain as day. It was time he stopped acting childish and spoke to Esme. He needed to tell her the truth about his feelings and hopefully she still felt the same.

Erik stood and bent at the waist blowing out breaths. It was possible he'd ruined any opportunity for a life with Esme.

He was a warrior, trained for battle. This was no different. He would fight for her... for them.

At a loud bird's call, he looked up at the sky.

On Skye, his father, who was an excellent swimmer, had taken both him and his brother and taught them to swim and to fish. The memories Erik treasured the most were those times when he'd gone fishing, hunting, and swimming with his father—alone—just the two of them.

The child he'd created with Esme deserved a father like his. One that took time despite working all day to teach his sons skills that would help them survive and provide for their own families one day.

"Ye will be a great warrior one day," his father had told him as he and his brother played with wooden swords his father had carved for them. "Ye will be a fighter who defends his people." Those words spoken with so much pride had been permanently etched into his soul.

Now he had the same opportunity. And he would not give up until Esme agreed to marry him and allow him to raise the bairn with her.

At the decision, it was as if a huge boulder was lifted from Erik's shoulders. Now he had to come up with a plan. Every warrior knew that in order to win a battle, one had to have a plan in place. Where to be, when to approach, and how to fight.

His steed snorted as if making fun of him and Erik turned to the animal. "Ye must be hungry. Let us return to camp. I have much to do."

CHAPTER NINETEEN

I T HAD BEEN three days since Esme had seen Erik and with each morning that passed, she felt better. Unfortunately, she could not keep from thinking of him. The beauty of his light blue eyes and the smile that played along his full lips. She'd regretted sending him away, but at the same time, he'd stayed from her for so long that it was hurtful.

"Esme?" Laith walked into the front room. "How fare ye?"

"I am well as ye can see." She continued sweeping the floor taking pride in their home and keeping it tidy. "I plan to go to the square in a bit. We need to purchase some meat for dinner."

"Aye, I tire of mutton," Laith replied. "I am going to Taernsby tomorrow. Do not forget."

Laith had been delighted when a group of men planned to travel there and had invited him along. It was obvious the people of Creag were enjoying their newfound freedom and were exploring the isle to seek new ways to make coin. The trip to Taernsby was to sell wares, but also to learn about farming. A peddler had told them of lush crops farmed there and it had awakened their curiosity.

"Be sure to stay with the group. Do not go off on yer own. We are not familiar with the way there and back and it is easy to get lost."

Laith nodded while counting the arrows in the two baskets he'd filled. "I will make a few more today." With a smile on his face, he went to the shed at the back of the house where he worked.

THE NEXT DAY, she once again made Laith promise to remain with the group and not stray. She would worry, of course, but he was now ten and four and felt as if he did not require so much of her attention.

Laith was very responsible and carefully thought things through before doing anything. If Esme were honest, he was the more levelheaded of the two of them.

Once the men departed on horseback and in Laith's case leading a wagon on which most of the wares they would sell were being carried, Esme said a quick prayer of blessing and went inside.

In the few days that Laith would be gone, she would take advantage and make clothing for the bairn. She'd spun wool to make blankets and had washed and rewashed linen to ensure it was soft to use to make gowns and swaddling blankets. She'd even gone so far as to dye thread in order to try her hand at embroidering the edges of the cloths.

She lifted the soft fabric and held it against her chest. "Ye will be so loved wee one. I promise to take care of ye. Ye will never suffer as I did."

There were knocks at the front door and Esme frowned. Not in the mood to be disturbed, she considered not opening it.

It wasn't Lattie since she never knocked. It could be she was needed for something. One of the things she'd decided upon moving into the house was to make every effort to be part of the community and help whenever needed.

After carefully placing the fabric on the table, she went to the door. To her shock, it was Erik who filled the doorway, a look of panic across his handsome features.

"What happens?" Esme asked trying to look around him. "Did something happen to Laith?"

"Who?" He shook his head. "Yer brother… no. That is not why I am here."

She let out a breath. "Ye look as if ye've seen a ghost. Whatever ye have to say must be bad news."

Despite not wishing to spend time alone with him, neither did she wish for the curious villagers to see him at her door. Esme moved back to allow him to enter.

"Esme," Erik started, meeting her gaze. "I-I… Are…" He swallowed visibly.

Panic rose within her. He was trying to tell her something so horrible even he—a fearless warrior—was having trouble saying it.

She grabbed the front of his tunic and pulled him forward and then pushed him backward. "Tell me!"

He blinked. "It is just that I do not know how to say what I wish to say. My words keep getting mixed up."

If ever she wanted to hit someone it was then. "Whatever it is just say it."

"I love ye."

It took several beats before she realized what he'd said. The formidable warrior stood before her looking uncertain and perhaps a bit scared. Was he toying with her?

"What do ye mean, ye love me?" Esme asked. "Ye have not

come to see about me in many weeks. Then suddenly ye say this."

His uncertain gaze met hers. "Ye repeatedly told me ye didna wish to see me. Ye want to be only with Laith. That ye do not need me."

Something in her chest tightened at his words. She had repeated the words to him, but it was because she expected that he did not plan to remain with her.

"I-I do wish to be with ye. But I do not trust that ye will remain. I am but a simple village girl with little knowledge of anything outside this village."

Tentatively, he reached for her hand. The feel of his large, calloused hand over hers sent tingles of awareness up her spine. "I am but a simple soldier for the laird. I have little to offer ye more than my heart, my body, and my promise to work hard to support ye, the bairn, and yer brother."

At the mention of the bairn, she snatched her hand away. "What do ye mean bairn?"

"Graeme, the healer, he suspects ye are with child. Whether ye are or not, I meant what I just said, Esme. I love ye. I wish to be with ye."

She glanced at the cloth on the table and considered whether it would be best to tell him the truth or not.

"How can I fully trust what ye say is true? Why did ye wait so long?"

"The laird's visit and having to travel back and forth to Taernsby to see about the matter of the men who fought against us. Then there was the issue of my men dividing. Some returned to the keep, while others remained. Torac and I had to assign duties to those left, we are few in number now, therefore, we each have to perform patrols and such daily."

He continued, "Ye are the first thing I think about each morning. I worry about what ye are doing. Knowing ye have been ill was killing me. Not able to see about ye."

Her body gave way and she fell forward onto his chest, her face pressed into the rough fabric of his tunic. When his strong arms came around her, Esme let out a long-held breath. A sense of security and safety filled her from head to toe.

Could this be true? Was she to wake and find that it was all a dream?

"Erik. I do love ye. But also I am scared." Esme lifted her face to look at him. "Tell me this is not a dream."

He kissed her gently. His lips brushed over hers in a way that drove her mad with anticipation of wanting more—needing—more.

When he straightened, she was both relieved and disappointed.

"Come sit. Let us talk." He pulled her to the table, and they each took a seat. Erik met her gaze. "Are ye expecting my bairn?"

Esme nodded, heat flushing her face. "Aye. I am expecting yer child."

The wide smile that split his face made her smile in return. "Are ye glad about it?"

"I am."

She pressed her lips together. "What do ye want to do?"

Erik took her hands and lifted them to his mouth, kissing each one while meeting her gaze. "That is what we must decide. I gave my word to remain in the laird's service at the camp. I must live there or nearby. I will ask the laird for permission to build us a home near the camp and ye and Laith can come to live with me."

Esme had not considered Laith. "I have nae told him as yet. I was waiting."

"I understand," Erik replied. "It is yer decision when ye wish to tell him. For now, can we just say we are to be married?"

At this Esme's eyes rounded. "Marry?"

"A child should be born to a married mother and father, 'tis how I was raised," Erik stated with a firm tone. "I hope that ye agree."

Too overwhelmed with happiness to speak, Esme nodded.

"We can go speak to the vicar today and be married right away." Erik met her gaze, the uncertainty returning. "If ye wish."

"I do wish to marry ye. Can we wait and speak to the vicar another day?" Esme asked. "I must get my thoughts in order."

"Do ye think to change yer mind?"

Esme stood and walked around the table to sit on his lap. Wrapping her arms around his neck, she nuzzled into his hair. She had missed his scent so. "I will not change my mind."

"Very well. I suppose I should go." Erik looked about the house. "I will build us one that is nicer."

Esme could not help but smile. "Can ye remain a bit longer?"

"Just a bit. I am supposed to be on patrol. I have to return by last meal. If one of my men did what I am doing, he would be disciplined."

Looking down into her eyes, he took her mouth with his. Although sweet, there was no passion in his kiss. Esme wondered if he was being gentle on purpose. She considered that perhaps it was best not to question or think too much but allow herself to enjoy the moment. The feel of his arms around her, his strong body against hers, and the steady heartbeat beneath her ear as she pressed her head against his chest.

When he stood, it was obvious he had to force himself to leave. Holding her hand until he reached the door, he pressed one more kiss on her lips. "I will return tomorrow."

THE NEXT DAY, Erik arrived earlier than expected. He had brought with him a sack that contained fruits, cabbages, carrots, and onions. And on a string, he had two skinned rabbits.

"Graeme says ye must eat well. To ensure ye stay healthy. Did ye feel sick this morning?"

Esme chuckled. "Thank the healer for me. I appreciate the food, but I have a rather lush garden, so there is no need to continue to bring me food. However, I am grateful."

After placing the items on the table, he went to her and hugged her close. "I kept thinking yesterday did not happen and that I dreamt it," he admitted. "I told Torac I would be here all day."

When he kissed her, again it was gentle and quick. Esme frowned at his back when he went to the table, found a knife, and began to cut the vegetables he'd brought.

"Are ye cooking?" Esme asked intrigued.

"Aye," he said. Esme stood at the end of the table looking on as he chopped, washed, and placed everything into a pot. Then he went to the hearth and stoked the fire to get it going. Once he placed the pot on the iron rod, he swung it to sit over the flames.

"Pull it back a bit, so it does not overboil too quickly," Esme said entertained by what he did.

Once that was done, he cleaned up the waste and put it into the pail of food that would be fed to her goats.

He looked to her. "When should we go speak to the vicar?"

Esme closed the distance between them. "Why are ye being so careful?"

"I am not being careful." He visibly swallowed.

Narrowing her eyes, Esme studied him. "Are ye doing all of this because of honor? Because ye feel as if ye should?"

"No." Erik shook his head. "I meant what I said. Believe me. I do love ye, Esme."

"Show me." She stood before him, her chest heaving in fear. If he did not prove to love her with his body and with his touch, she would let him go. It would not be fair to keep a man tied to her out of duty.

Erik brought her against him. His mouth crushing hers with force, his hands yanking at her clothes with desperation, not caring even when her dress tore. She gasped at finding he'd undressed her completely in a matter of seconds.

With just as much impatience, he yanked his own clothing off. When fully naked he pulled her against him and again took her mouth with his.

Esme lost her ability to breathe, between his kisses and the feel of his hands running down her back to cup her bottom and lift her up from the floor.

"I need ye," Erik said, his heated words combined with his hot breath at her ear. Instantly Esme became consumed with need. Not wishing to wait a moment longer. She was filled with the rawest sensation that she'd ever experienced.

"Aye," she said, clinging to him as he walked her to the nearest bed. She didn't care about anything other than being with Erik, being claimed by him, and sensing how he truly felt.

Upon laying her on the bed, he then climbed over her. His gaze met hers. "I not only desire ye, but I want ye to be mine."

She pulled him down to kiss her, wanting to feel his weight come over her. It was perfect. Not only the slow caresses of his hands over her heated skin but the trail of kisses from her mouth to her shoulder.

Settling between her legs, Erik entered her slowly and her body welcomed him fully. Esme moaned at how perfect it felt.

She'd not allowed herself to believe they would ever be together like this again. But now that it was happening, the emotions and sensations threatened to overcome her.

"I do not know what to feel," Esme admitted.

"Become lost with me," Erik replied. In a steady rhythm, he pulled out and pushed back in until fully seated. The more he drove in and out, the more she desired it. It was like a never-ending cycle of want and desire.

When she crested, Esme cried out, tears spilling down her cheeks. For a few moments, it was as if they were alone in the world. Slowly the sounds of Erik's moans as he too found his release permeated through the fog of her own pleasure.

"THE STEW IS bubbling," Esme said as she played with the ends of Erik's hair. "It will boil over if not tended to." She was thoroughly enjoying the fact Erik was cooking a meal for her.

He kissed her and looked into her eyes. "Do not move."

The picture of him naked moving the pot from the fire was

as mouthwatering as the aroma of the food. Erik smiled when he caught her looking.

"I like that ye are bold in yer admiration."

Esme pretended to be shocked. "I was looking at the pot. It smells good."

"Mmm," he replied then returned to the bed. "We should eat and then go see the vicar. I must return to the camp in the morning."

Although she wanted to marry Erik more than anything, she hated that Laith would not be present for it.

"Can we wait?"

Erik's look of panic made her reach for him. He climbed back into the bed, and she snuggled against his chest.

"It is just that I wish to have Laith, Lattie, and her family present when we marry. I wish to invite Colin and his wife as well."

"If that is what ye wish, then I agree. I will ask Torac and Struan to come and be my witnesses."

Esme kissed his neck. "I am hungry."

"For?" Erik rolled her onto her back and trailed kisses down her neck until reaching her breasts where he took one rosy tip in his mouth and then the other until she was shaking with want.

This time when he took her, he was gentle, the lovemaking slow.

"Erik?" Esme gasped. "I need ye to do something . . . more."

He chuckled, then withdrew and rolled her onto her stomach. "Up on yer knees, lass."

She lifted to her knees and gasped when he entered her

from behind. It was wonderfully pleasing as he thrust into her. Just as she was near release, something held her back and she pushed back against his strokes needing more.

Erik reached around her and stroked between the folds of her sex. Esme thought she would faint when a streak of heat traveled up and down her body making her shake and cry out as she lost control.

"THE FOOD IS going to be cold," Erik said as he lazily caressed her arm.

Fully spent, Esme lay across his chest, her eyes closed and body feeling languid. "I am hungry."

"Come get up."

They ate the stew, which was still warm, enjoying kisses in between bites.

It was the most wonderful day of her life.

"I STILL DO not know why ye are in such a hurry to marry," Laith complained, his face filled with worry. "Are ye sure about this Esme?"

She'd already dressed and waited for Lattie to arrive so they could walk to the small village chapel together.

Esme kissed her brother's cheek. "I have been telling ye for several days. Erik spoke to ye and ye said to be glad that we marry." Although Laith's concern was endearing, she wanted to shake him for bringing up doubts on the very day of the wedding.

"It is just that I do not understand why ye and he cannot

wait. There has been no courtship. Ye should be courted."

She let out a breath. "Laith. I wish to marry Erik. We love each other. There is no need to wait. Besides, do ye not wish for yer niece or nephew to be born into a home with both parents?"

At first Laith huffed, then upon realizing what she alluded to, his eyes widened. "We should hurry." He walked to the door and opened it. "Where are Ian and Lattie?"

To Esme's surprise, there were more guests than she had expected. Not only were the tavern owner and his wife there, but most of the vendors from the village square and their families attended the wedding as well.

There were so many well-wishers they spilled out of the chapel and upon the vicar declaring them husband and wife great cheers arose from inside and out.

Esme cried in delight at the sight of the long tables set up in the village square laden with food that all the families had brought in celebration. A large boar was roasted by Erik's men, who had refused to remain behind.

Ale was provided by Colin and musicians played lively tunes. Esme couldn't have asked for a more perfect wedding day.

Everyone went silent as Ian stood up on the small stand where the band played. He scanned the group of people gathered until meeting Esme's gaze.

"Esme, yer marriage ceremony brought us together this day. We are humbled by yer kindness and yer forgiveness, despite the fact that most of us stood by while the council and their sons mistreated ye and Laith. Ye and Erik are always welcome here and we are so grateful that ye share this day with us."

There were cheers and a few tears by some women who were clearly saddened by the reminder of their past actions. But mostly there was joy, and one by one people came to her and Erik to congratulate them, some with gifts.

"THIS WAS CERTAINLY not the private quiet wedding ye wished for," Erik said that night as they lay in bed. Laith had been invited to spend a pair of nights at Lattie's house to give the couple some time alone.

They'd decided she and Laith would remain in the village. Erik would begin building their new home and come there every few days, or Esme would go see him on her way to Welland. Although he didn't like her continuing to sell baskets, she insisted it made her happy to keep busy.

"I cannot wait to live together. I will miss ye the days ye are away," Esme said.

Erik pressed a kiss to her temple. "I look forward to the warm welcomes when I arrive."

They chuckled at his comment, falling asleep moments later exhausted from the eventful day.

CHAPTER TWENTY

TORAC RODE FROM the camp toward the farmlands. It was a warm day as the season turned toward summer. The patrols had become monotonous as of late. Now that there were no threats from the village, he found little purpose in his duties. There were little squabbles here and there that he and Erik were called to help with, but for the most part, it had been peaceful in the last months.

The laird had agreed to gift Erik and Esme a plot of land that bordered both the creek and forest. It was just a few minutes on horseback to the camp. The warriors had kept busy helping Erik build a large cottage, which was turning out to be quite grand.

Now Erik lived there, leaving him, Struan, Balgair, and Graeme to share the quarters set aside for the leadership.

His thoughts were disrupted when a woman ran across his path, her long reddish hair flowing behind her like a banner.

"Wait!" Torac called out to her. "Is something wrong?"

She looked over her shoulder and upon seeing him darted into the field and disappeared.

Torac dismounted and ran after her. It was obvious the woman was under distress. Had someone attacked her?

The plants were up to his shoulders, he had to push them away as he hurried forward. Then stopping to listen for sounds of someone else. It was silent. She must have stopped and was hiding.

"I do not mean ye harm," Torac called out. "Is something wrong?"

Silence.

"If ye require anything, I am called Torac. I will be riding past here later today."

He walked back to his steed unable to shake the feeling that something was wrong. Why had the woman run away and hid?

Upon mounting, he studied the field for a long time before urging his mount forward. He would stop at the nearest farm and ask about her.

A man stood out at the end of a field peering up at the sky. Upon noticing Torac, he watched him approach.

"Guard to the laird, aye?" the man asked. "Ye have been a great help to us."

"I am," Torac said and dismounted. "What do ye search for?"

At his question, the older man shook his head. "I am hoping for rain. 'Tis been almost a sennight without it."

"I saw a woman," Torac began noticing the man tense. "She seemed distressed. She was running and hid upon seeing me."

The farmer scanned his fields. "The only woman who would be out and about alone is Leana MacKern, she lives across the way with her father. She gathers herbs and such."

"Does she have long reddish hair?"

"Aye that is her," the farmer chuckled. "A bit daft."

"Daft?" Torac looked over to the fields. The woman he'd

caught a glimpse of looked quite lovely. It was a shame if she wasn't all there.

"Perhaps not daft," the farmer continued, seeming to enjoy having someone to talk with. "Timid. Will nae look ye in the eye, nor talk."

They spoke for a bit longer while Torac kept looking toward the field. If the lass hid, she was quite patient.

Just as he mounted, he caught sight of the lass. She was in the trees carrying a basket and every so often bending over to pick something up.

Torac dismounted and quietly went up behind her. It wasn't that he wished to scare her, but more that he was intrigued by the thought of a woman so lovely not being right of mind.

"Leana?" he whispered, and she whirled around, eyes wide and mouth open. He was close enough to see that her eyes were a bright green and there was a sprinkling of freckles across her pert nose.

Her plump lips were a bright pink, and her hair was like a silken curtain.

"Ouch!" Torac shouted when she slapped him across the face with a thin reed. Just as she was about to dash away, he grabbed her arm.

"Why did ye do that?" he asked doing his best to ignore the fact that when her shawl slipped, the flimsy excuse for a blouse gave a very precise outline of her ample breasts.

"Let me go," she whispered, seeming on the brink of tears. "P-please."

"I will but first ye should apologize."

"I-I am s-sorry." Her tear-filled wide eyes met his. "P-please." She tugged trying to release her arm, but he held it, not wishing for her to dash away.

At noticing she was shaking, Torac felt bad. "I did not mean to startle ye. It is I who should apologize."

She hung her head, not looking at him, and nodded.

"Ye should not be alone in the forest. Harm could befall ye." He released her arm, and she took a step backward seeming to be at a loss as what to do.

Torac picked up her basket and even the reed she'd struck him with and held them out to her.

She grabbed the items and quick as a hare she dashed away, disappearing into the woods.

When he touched the side of his face, Torac flinched. He would have a mark that would last a few days at least.

Upon mounting he continued on patrol, the woman Leana forefront on his mind.

Torac, Book 2 in the Guards of Clan Ross series

Does he bring salvation or devastation?

On the brink of hanging up his sword for good, seasoned warrior Torac Bratton returns to action for a beautiful, endangered lass.

Accused of murder, Leana MacKern has no choice but to **trust the handsome warrior, Torac.**

With secrets of his own, **Torac holds her heart and her fate in his hands.**

Find out why thousands of readers have fallen in love with Hildie McQueen's brave highlanders. You'll be up all night to finish this tale of finding love amidst the darkest danger.

Order **TORAC** today

A Note to Readers

Let's get to know one another,

Sign up for my newsletter and get a free Clan Ross story!

Newsletter Link: https://bit.ly/3vSEbYY

I sent out my newsletter monthly which includes book news, giveaways and sneak peeks!

About the Author

Enticing. Engaging. Romance.

USA Today Bestselling Author Hildie McQueen writes strong brooding alphas who meet their match in feisty brave heroines. If you like stories with a mixture of passion, drama, and humor, you will love Hildie's storytelling where love wins every single time!

A fan of all things pink, Paris, and four-legged creatures, Hildie resides in eastern Georgia, USA, with her super-hero husband Kurt and three little yappy dogs.

Visit her website at www.hildiemcqueen.com.

Printed in Great Britain
by Amazon

16903436R00129